BARBAR

Harlequin Presents and bestselling author
Charlotte Lamb welcome you to the world of
Barbary Wharf.

In this fascinating saga, you'll experience all the
intrigue and glamour of the international world
of journalism. You'll watch the inner workings
of a newsroom, share the secrets discussed behind closed doors, travel to the most thrilling
cities in the world. Join the players in this high-
stakes game as they gamble for the biggest prize
of all—true love.

You've met Nick Caspian and Gina Tyrrell,
whose dramatic story of passion and heartache
unfolds throughout this series. And you've followed the relationships of three couples—Hazel
Forbes and Piet van Leyden, Roz Amery and
Daniel Bruneille, and Irena Olivero and
Esteban Sebastian—as each fell in love. Now
join Valerie Knight and Gib Collingwood to discover if it *is* possible to combine business with
pleasure.

Don't miss these unforgettable romantic adven-
tures each month in Harlequin Presents—the
bestselling romance fiction series in the world.

The Editors

THE SENTINEL

THE CHILD IS NOT MINE
MAC CAMERON DENIES PATERNITY

LONDON—Actor Mac Cameron is threatening to bring legal action against the *Sentinel* and feature writer Valerie Knight after the paper published a story alleging that Mr. Cameron is the father of Molly Green's unborn child.

"The story is false," Mr. Cameron claimed yesterday. He issued the statement at a news conference called by his lawyers to deny the report. Mr. Cameron acknowledged that he had been dating Ms. Green in past months, but he denied that the baby is his.

"I didn't know the *Sentinel* was in the rumormongering business," he said. "If Ms. Knight feels the need to probe into everyone else's love life, perhaps it's time she got one of her own. When the baby is born I will happily submit to a blood test. In the mean-time, my lawyers tell me we have an excellent case for libel."

Ms. Knight and counsel for the *Sentinel* said they stand by her story and that a retraction will not be printed.

BURNING THE CANDLE AT BOTH ENDS?

LONDON—Gina Tyrrell, acting head of the *Sentinel,* was seen leaving the home of actor Mac Cameron early this morning by one of the paper's staff reporters. Ms. Tyrrell had attended the previous evening's performance of the hit musical starring Mr. Cameron. Was Ms. Tyrrell simply trying to reason with Mr. Cameron and convince him not to launch a libel suit against the *Sentinel,* or are Ms. Tyrrell and Mr. Cameron more than just friends? And where does this leave Nick Caspian, the man most recently linked to Ms. Tyrrell?

Charlotte Lamb

Playing Hard To Get

BARBARY WHARF

Harlequin Books

TORONTO • NEW YORK • LONDON
AMSTERDAM • PARIS • SYDNEY • HAMBURG
STOCKHOLM • ATHENS • TOKYO • MILAN
MADRID • WARSAW • BUDAPEST • AUCKLAND

Harlequin Presents first edition January 1993
ISBN 0-373-11522-9

Original hardcover edition published in 1992
by Mills & Boon Limited

PLAYING HARD TO GET

BARBARY WHARF

For more than one hundred years, London's Fleet Street has been the heartbeat of Britain's major newspaper and magazine industries. But decaying buildings and the high cost of inner-city real estate have forced many companies to relocate dockside, down by the Thames River.

The owner of one such company, Sir George Tyrrell, had a dream, a vision of leading his newspaper, the *Sentinel*, into the twenty-first century with a huge, ultramodern complex called Barbary Wharf. But without additional money and time, the dream—and perhaps even the newspaper—will die.

Enter Nick Caspian, international media tycoon. The man with all the money, desire and the means to take over the *Sentinel*. But will he change the paper beyond recognition? Will he change the life of Gina Tyrrell, a woman who understands his desires?

And what of the people behind the scenes at the *Sentinel*? Not only does feature writer Valerie Knight have to dodge persistent Gib Collingwood, now she's faced with a potential lawsuit. And the *Sentinel*'s lawyer, Guy Faulkner, isn't making things any easier—or is he? His meetings with Valerie have taken on a decidedly unprofessional flavor....

BARBARY WHARF

CAST OF CHARACTERS

Valerie Knight—Award-winning feature writer. Valerie has dedicated her writing to unmasking treachery of any sort, particularly romantic betrayal. Following the bitter divorce of her parents, she is adamant she will never get involved with a married man—no matter how she feels about him.

Gib Collingwood—Charming but cheeky finance editor. Recently divorced, he is now attempting to woo Valerie Knight, a woman he's long been attracted to. Gib's plans don't always work out as he expects.

Gina Tyrrell—The young widow of Sir George Tyrrell's beloved grandson. Devastated by her husband's death, she devoted herself entirely to Sir George's well-being. And now she will devote herself entirely to his paper, the *Sentinel*.

Nick Caspian—International media tycoon with playboy reputation. Owns and operates newspapers all over Europe, and has now set his sights on Britain—starting with the *Sentinel*.

Guy Faulkner—The *Sentinel*'s sophisticated lawyer. He has recently realized that his career has become his whole life. It's time to devote some attention to outside pursuits—it's time to fall in love.

Mac Cameron—International star of stage and screen. Mac has the reputation of being a merciless lady-killer who, rumor has it, will stop at nothing to achieve his goal.

CHAPTER ONE

VALERIE KNIGHT walked into Barbary Wharf just after eleven on a hot morning towards the end of August, wishing she could have stayed in bed. She had been up until the early hours at a first-night party. It hadn't been easy to get up when her alarm shrilled, but she had picked up any amount of hot gossip which she must write up for tomorrow's paper before another paper beat her to it.

Blonde, with a curvy, sexy figure, and strikingly unusual eyes so blue as to be violet, Valerie liked to give everyone the impression she was a butterfly, skimming over the surface of life, having lots of fun and taking nothing seriously. The truth was she worked hard at her job and had a strong will. However little sleep she had the night before, she was at work next day in good time to keep appointments, interview people, or turn in copy for next day's paper, which was why she was now the *Sentinel*'s top feature writer.

While she was waiting impatiently for a lift to arrive she glanced out through the glass doors into the plaza gardens. Roberto Torelli, in a clean white apron, stood in the doorway of the snack bar enjoying the sunlight, lucky man. Overhead the sky was blue and cloudless—what a waste being shut indoors on a day like this! Today was Friday, though; if the weather didn't change before the weekend, maybe she would be able to get in some sunbathing?

A group of men came in from the plaza; recognising one of them, Valerie turned away again, but too late. He had seen her.

'Don't tell me you're just arriving!' he mocked, coming up behind her.

'I won't, then.' Valerie jabbed the lift button again. All the lifts appeared to be stuck on upper floors. Wouldn't you know it, just when you desperately needed one!

'I wish I had your job. I've been here since nine.'

'And I was working until three o'clock this morning!' she snapped. Did he have to stand so close, invading her body space?

He leaned even closer. 'I like the perfume—what is it?'

'I can't remember.' It was true; her mind was a blank, he had that effect on her. He was an infuriating man.

'What were you doing until three this morning?' he asked, and she had to think hard to remember, which made her angry, because she resented having her wits scrambled this way.

'I was at a party.' She jabbed the lift button again.

'With?'

The curt question made her nerves jump and she snapped back at him.

'Half Fleet Street. Wessex Studios threw a huge party to get pre-publicity for *Good Living*, their latest film.' It was a safe subject so she talked on about it. 'All the stars were there—Christa Nordstrom, Lee Palmer and Bianca Valence—we even had a film show; they showed us a clip from the film, which is still being edited. There was caviare and smoked salmon and champagne; it was quite a party.'

To her relief the lift arrived a second later, she stopped talking and walked quickly into it. Gilbey Collingwood

followed, but the rest of his party had given up waiting
and taken the stairs, which meant that when the lift doors
shut again Valerie was alone with him.

She felt that familiar nervous tremor inside her chest
and wanted to scream. It was inexplicable. She didn't
even like him. All she wanted was for him to leave her
alone. So how on earth did he manage to cause these
odd symptoms?

'I've been trying to talk to you all week, but you're
never in your office,' he drawled, leaning on the steel
wall of the lift with one hand, and leaning over, far too
close to her. He had a very physical presence, and she
couldn't pretend she wasn't aware of him. A tall man,
he was an athlete, with rugged features, broad shoulders,
and long, slim legs. His accountant's City suit couldn't
hide the powerful body under it, or make him look like
the others who worked with him, grey, dull men often
turning prematurely bald.

He was popular with his colleagues, though. Everyone
seemed to know him, and called him Gib. He made them
laugh, and he was something of a hero because from
the minute he joined the *Sentinel* he had been a leading
light in the newspaper's sporting club.

He had played rugger for the club; he swam for it,
and ran in their annual marathon, often coming among
the first half-dozen to finish. He had a lot of friends,
not to mention girls eager to get his attention.

Valerie was not one of them. In fact, she avoided him
whenever she could. If he would only let her!

'I've had a very busy week. I've been out doing interviews almost every day.' Valerie slid sideways in an
effort to escape him, but he shifted too.

'Well, now I've got you to myself, which do you want
first—the good news or the bad news?'

She looked up blankly. 'What?'

'Maybe we had better start with the good news. My divorce came through last Monday.' He spoke coolly, but he was watching her with the sharp-eyed alertness of a cat at a mousehole. 'I'm a free man again,' he said.

Valerie stiffened and quickly looked away. So he really had got divorced? She hadn't quite believed he was telling the truth when he'd claimed to be waiting for his divorce to be made final. Men were always talking about leaving their wives, getting divorced; mostly they did not mean a word of it.

'Do I say I'm sorry, or congratulate you?' she asked lightly.

'I told you, my marriage has been over for a long time,' Gib said with a sharp edge to his voice, as if irritated. 'My wife went to Australia years ago and has been living with another man over there. Now it's a legal fact, that's all. I'm free—and Clare, my ex-wife, remarried on Tuesday.'

'On Tuesday?' Valerie's eyes flew open again, in disbelief. 'But didn't you say the divorce only came through on Monday?'

'She was in a hurry,' he drily said.

'She must have been!'

'Well, it is understandable. She's expecting a baby and wanted to marry before it appeared. It's due any time.'

That did explain the need for hurry, but Valerie said, 'I don't know why she bothered. After all, is there any point in taking vows you didn't keep the first time around?'

Gib's brows met and he gave her an angrily glinting look. 'Clare and I were human. Or don't you understand what that means, Valerie? I know you're a perfectionist, but some of us can't reach your heady heights. Clare and I made a mistake, we rushed into marriage before we really knew each other; it happens all the time.

This time she hasn't rushed into it, she's been living with him for some years and she's sure it is going to last.'

'You're very tolerant!' Valerie's tone was tart, she hadn't liked the way he'd made fun of her just now. It was true she was a perfectionist, and she saw nothing to apologise for in that. When she married she would make very sure it was perfect, and would last a lifetime.

Gib's wide, flexible mouth twisted in irony as if he could read her thoughts. 'Why shouldn't I be? Oh, I know you despise tolerance—you see it as a weakness, don't you?'

'Stop putting words in my mouth!' she snapped. 'I can speak for myself if I want to, thanks!'

He shrugged. 'Well, my marriage broke up a long time ago, I was bitter for a while, but now I'm over it I wish her luck.'

The lift had stopped at the editorial floor. She walked out, and Gib followed her. She gave him a sideways look.

'You're on the wrong floor.'

'I haven't told you the bad news yet.'

'I'm not sure I want to hear it,' she muttered. 'Bad news can always wait.'

'Well, maybe you already know,' drawled Gib, pushing back his thick, dark brown hair with one hand. 'About Esteban...'

'What about Esteban?' she asked, startled. 'He's in Paris at the moment, at some marketing conference.'

Esteban Sebastian was the marketing director of the newspaper, and Valerie had been attracted to his dark, Spanish good looks from the minute she first saw him. When they were together, they made a striking pair— Esteban so dark, and Valerie so fair. She enjoyed seeing people stare at them. She wasn't actually in love with Esteban, but she thought she could fall in love with him; he was exactly the type of man she wanted to marry.

Unlike Gilbey Collingwood, Esteban was serious, thoughtful, very courteous and had a secret romantic streak which she had glimpsed from the beginning. She loved men who gave you red roses and treated you as if you were made of porcelain; it made her feel very feminine. If Esteban got married, it would be for ever, and he would make a wonderful husband.

'He hasn't had an accident?' she asked anxiously. Esteban could have made the mistake of trying to cross a busy Paris street on a pedestrian crossing and been mown down by a speeding car. Valerie had long ago given up trying to use pedestrian crossings in France—drivers simply drove right over you if you didn't leap out of their way in time.

'Not exactly! He's got engaged!' Gib said softly, his hazel eyes intent on her face.

For a second she stared at him, her eyes darkening almost to purple; then she gave a short laugh. 'Oh, very funny!'

'It isn't a joke,' Gib said. 'He's going to marry Irena— Roz Amery's little half-sister.'

'Irena?' repeated Valerie flatly, remembering the little girl, who had worked briefly in the translation department of the paper. Irena had been so young that she couldn't believe Esteban would ever take her seriously! She had hardly been a great beauty, either, with her straight brown hair and those wide, childlike eyes. She hadn't even had a figure, she had been far too small and skinny. 'Don't be ridiculous! She's just a teenager!' Valerie said, and got a straight, sharp stare from Gilbey Collingwood.

'Valerie, it's true,' he said in a tone she couldn't laugh off.

Their eyes met and held, and she flushed at the look in his eyes. He was telling her the truth, she realised in shock, and then she bristled—was that pity in his eyes? How dared he look at her like that?

'She's a student at the Sorbonne, in Paris,' said Gib quietly. 'When she finished her summer job here, she went back to university, and then, while Esteban was over there, at this conference, he talked to Des Amery. You know how formal Spaniards can be! Esteban wanted her father's permission to ask her to marry him, and apparently Des gave them his blessing.'

'How do you know all this?' Valerie asked half angrily.

'They had an engagement party in Paris, and a lot of Caspian International people were invited. Jack Summers, Esteban's deputy, was at the marketing conference, so he went to the party. He flew back this morning, and I just had coffee with him. Esteban is still in Paris. It seems Esteban plans to move back to Madrid—he doesn't feel at home in London—but he'll wait until Irena has finished her last year at the Sorbonne, then they'll get married. Jack is hoping to get his job when he goes, of course.'

While he was talking, Valerie had been struggling with a cocktail of reaction: shock, incredulity, wounded pride. Everyone on the *Sentinel* knew that she was interested in Esteban, people would be watching her, whispering, wondering how badly she had been hurt—and knowing that made her feel far worse. Valerie hated the thought of being pitied.

She managed to give Gib a cool smile. 'Well, it sounds more like good news than bad to me.'

There was a flicker of admiration or amusement in his eyes; she didn't care which it was, she just wanted to get away from him. At that instant, to her relief, she caught sight of the new features editor gesturing impatiently towards her from the other end of the room.

'I must go,' she said hurriedly. 'There's Colette waving at me.'

Without looking at him again, she walked away rapidly, through the busy newsroom, feeling Gib's hazel eyes fixed on her back. What had he been expecting? That she would break down and sob on his shoulder when he told her Esteban was going to marry someone else?

Thank heavens she hadn't got to the stage of letting herself care that deeply about Esteban. He had had all the qualities she was looking for, but Valerie was very, very cautious. She had almost decided to take Esteban seriously, but not quite yet. The only really serious damage was to her ego and her public image. She felt her face burn at the thought of what people might say. She had plenty of friends, but she knew she had enemies, too, who wouldn't be sorry to see her dumped by Esteban. Some of the plainer girls were unfriendly because they resented the way she looked; some of the men were hostile because she had turned them down at some time.

And if Gilbey Collingwood thought that he would have more of a chance with her now that Esteban was out of the running, he could forget it! She had told him over and over again that she wasn't interested, but he never gave up trying! Well, he had better get it into his head. She had no intention of getting involved with a man who took marriage as lightly as Gilbey Collingwood did.

It was odd, of course, that he pursued her with such unswerving determination, but she suspected that that was simply because she kept saying no! If she had accepted a date with him when they first met he would be chasing someone else by now. He was that sort of man, and not her type at all.

She knew what she wanted out of life—out of her career, out of love, out of marriage. Underneath her blonde hair and vivacious manner, Valerie Knight was serious about everything, and she had dreams she would die rather than confide to anyone. They certainly did not include Gilbey Collingwood.

She walked into Colette Tse's glass-walled little office and at once started talking. 'I know I'm late, but that party last night went on until three in the morning and——'

'Never mind that now,' Colette interrupted. 'That gossip item you filed, about Mac Cameron...'

Valerie's attention sharpened. 'I checked it out,' she quickly said. 'If you remember, I saw the night lawyer about it, and it was passed. The girl had a whole album of photos of them together on his yacht, in the Caribbean, last January, she gave us the two we used, and I saw a medical report. The girl's definitely pregnant, and it would have been conceived around the time she was on the yacht with Cameron.'

Colette shrugged. 'Well, his lawyers are threatening a lawsuit, and he's denying the whole thing. He says it isn't his baby.'

Valerie sat down on the edge of Colette's desk, suddenly weak-kneed. This was the nightmare scenario every journalist dreaded. Her career could be over if she got the *Sentinel* into a damaging lawsuit. 'He's got to be lying,' she thought aloud, her voice slightly shaky. 'I believed that girl; she was only twenty-one, and rather sweet.'

'Did you check with Cameron before you filed the story?'

Valerie shook her head. 'I couldn't get in touch with him. He was in Spain, filming.'

'But you tried?'

'I rang his home and his housekeeper said she didn't know when he would be back.'

'Mmm.' Colette had that bland, smiling, ambiguous expression Valerie had begun to recognise. You never quite knew what she was thinking, or if she was likely to support you in whatever battle you had to fight.

A tiny, slender woman in her early thirties, half-English, half-Chinese, she was an extraordinary mixture of each parent. She had an English sense of humour, and straight black hair, a quality of Oriental impassiveness, high cheekbones and olive skin, and wide blue eyes. She was also brilliant at her job.

She had been poached from one of the *Sentinel*'s rival papers, by their proprietor, Nick Caspian. Since he'd taken over running the *Sentinel*, the senior staff on the paper had changed several times. He moved people, transferred or sacked them, hired new staff, and promoted others, in search of the best possible line-up for the paper's new image.

The *Sentinel* had been one of the most respected quality national papers under the previous management, but it had had a very low circulation, making a large part of its income from expensive advertising, and Nick Caspian intended to boost sales by leaps and bounds, which was why he kept head-hunting successful journalists like Colette, even if it meant paying them large salaries.

Many of the older journalists who had been on the paper for years resented the way the *Sentinel* was changing, relentlessly moving down market in search of bigger sales. They sat in the wine-bar in the plaza downstairs complaining about the radical changes sweeping away the world they had known for years, and one by one they were leaving, either retiring or finding other jobs.

Valerie Knight, though, was typical of the sort of journalist Nick Caspian wanted on the paper; she suited the new style he was establishing, the bright, modern, jazzy writing he wanted, and she was ambitious. The idea of being the cause of a lawsuit appalled her.

'This is not turning out to be a good day!' she muttered. First, she had heard that Esteban was going to marry someone else—and now even her job was under threat. She hadn't even had any premonition as she'd travelled to work. All she had had was a faint headache after that party last night. If she had known what was waiting for her when she got to the office she would have stayed in bed.

'You had better get all your evidence together,' said Colette. 'There's a meeting at three o'clock today, up in Mr Caspian's office, and he wants to see the original photos and the photostat of the medical certificate, and your tape-recording of the interview with Molly Green.'

'You know, I did believe her,' Valerie said, frowning. 'She had the sort of face you do believe, and, after all, Mac Cameron is notorious for his affairs. Film fans throw themselves at him. It all fitted.'

'Maybe that's the trouble? Did it fit because it was a frame?' Colette sounded dry and Valerie grimaced.

'I suppose it could be.'

'Cameron has never denied one of his affairs before. In fact, he seems to enjoy his reputation as a stud. It certainly helps his film career, and in a few years he'll be coming up to the big four-oh, which is a watershed for most actors. Having some girlfriends keeps him looking young, and he flaunts them whenever he's out on a date.'

'None of them has produced a baby before,' Valerie pointed out. 'This time it could cost him a fortune, in child support.'

Colette slowly nodded. 'True. Well, bring all your evidence upstairs at three o'clock, and keep your fingers crossed that they decide to back you up.'

'Will you be there?' Valerie was uncertain where Colette stood.

'Of course. I'm responsible for what my staff write.' Colette's voice was expressionless—no way of guessing whether she meant to support Valerie or fling her to the wolves. She picked up a typed sheet of paper which Valerie recognised as the morning running list of possible items for tomorrow's paper. 'Did you pick up anything last night?'

'A few good gossip items,' Valerie said absently, her mind still on the threatened lawsuit.

'Then go and write them up, but don't risk using anything borderline. For the moment, everything you write will be double-checked by the lawyers. Go to lunch early. I want you in the office by half-past two at the latest, so that I can look over your evidence before we go upstairs to face the music.'

That sounded ominous. Valerie nodded bleakly, and went back to her desk. The first thing she did was find Molly Green's phone number and ring her. Molly's mother answered the phone, her voice chilling when Valerie gave her name.

'She's gone to Devon to stay with her cousin!'

'When will she be back?'

'No idea.'

Valerie paused, frowning. How much should she tell Molly's mother? 'Look, Mrs Green,' she said slowly, 'it's important that I talk to Molly...'

'Important for whom? You, of course! It won't do my Molly any good! You didn't do her any favours putting her in your paper! Just go away!'

She slammed the phone down and Valerie winced. Well, she would try again later, she decided, and across the long room caught sight of Daniel Bruneille, the foreign news editor. Daniel was living with Roz Amery, one of their foreign correspondents, and the half-sister of Irena, the girl Esteban was going to marry.

Valerie was reminded of the news Gilbey Collingwood had given her, and sighed. No, this really wasn't turning out to be one of her better days. What else could go wrong?

Daniel's dark eyes met hers and she saw from the look in them that he had heard about the lawsuit. No doubt it was all round Barbary Wharf by now! It was surprising that Gilbey Collingwood hadn't heard about it, or perhaps so far only senior editorial staff knew?

Gib worked on the business section of the paper, writing dull stuff about merchant banks and share issues, falling profits and bull or bear markets. He had started out as an accountant and worked for a City of London merchant bank for a while before turning journalist. With such a solid, serious background it was odd that he was far from being either.

She frowned. Why on earth was she thinking about him? How had Gilbey Collingwood got inside her head when she had far more disturbing things to think about?

She evicted him from her mind and went back to her desk. First, she switched on her computer, then got out of her bag her various notebooks and the tape machine on which she had recorded brief interviews, in quiet corners, at the party last night.

She flicked through it all, realising that much of it was risky material, sighed, and began to type a short piece on Wessex Studios into the computer, using the printed hand-out she had been sent beforehand by the publicity people from the studio. At least they couldn't sue her over their own material!

It took her three-quarters of an hour to finish work on the gossip items, then she went down to the plaza to buy a pre-packed salad lunch from Torelli's. It was blazing hot by now, so she walked into the riverside gardens, finding most of the benches occupied. London was enjoying a last summer heatwave. September began on Tuesday and autumn was on the way. Londoners were taking advantage of this weather while it was around. It could change at any minute. Which was why the gardens were full of people eating their lunch in the sunshine; something of a tradition already at Barbary Wharf. On Fridays some people had lunch in Pierre's, especially if they had just been paid, but others preferred to picnic, looking over the river.

Valerie found an empty bench under a tree and ate her salad with the little plastic fork Roberto had provided, drank her can of orange juice, and relaxed for a few minutes to watch a string of tarpaulin-covered barges slowly making their way towards Tower Bridge.

She would have liked to stay there all afternoon, but she had to get back, so with a sigh she got up to return to the office.

As she turned, she caught sight of Gilbey Collingwood coming down the garden steps. There was a girl beside him, talking to him. Valerie knew she had seen her somewhere before but couldn't place her. Slender, with a smooth chignon of golden-brown hair, she was wearing a summer dress, white, printed with poppies in vivid red. It was very striking and so was the girl who wore it.

Who was she? Valerie frowned, trying to remember, and at that instant the girl tripped over something on the path, and lurched forward. Gib grabbed her by the waist and hauled her upright again. She clutched his shirt, then looked up, laughing, at him. Gib grinned down at her, his hazel eyes full of charm. You would have been blind if you couldn't see the intimacy between them.

Valerie saw it, and felt a sharp jab behind her ribs, turning away angrily. What was the matter with her? It was no surprise, was it? Hadn't she always known he was a flirt? She had learnt to recognise his type when she was barely out of school, and had fallen hopelessly in love with a man who had hurt her badly. He had had all Gib's charm and attraction, and he hadn't meant a word he said, either.

Valerie walked back into Barbary Wharf and took the lift up to Editorial, brooding over the way Gib had looked at the other girl.

Thank heavens she had never weakened, let him talk her into a date! She almost had from time to time. He was a very attractive man, after all. But the habit of wariness had saved her from making a complete fool of herself, and from now on Gilbey Collingwood wasn't getting within a mile of her.

Where had she seen the other girl, though? Maybe she worked with Gib, on business news?

At five to three that afternoon, Valerie and Colette Tse walked into Nick Caspian's secretary's office. Hazel van Leyden was on the phone and looked up, gave them a polite, rather distant little smile and gestured for them to take a seat, while continuing with her conversation.

'Yes, Mr Lincoln, that will be quite convenient. Yes, at three o'clock next Tuesday afternoon. No, check in at Reception and someone will come down to meet you. Not at all—thank *you*. Goodbye.'

She put the phone down and turned towards them, giving them another of those automatic, polite smiles which were not mirrored in her grey eyes.

'Mr Caspian is talking to the lawyers; he'll buzz when he wants you to join them. I'm sure he won't keep you waiting much longer.'

Hazel was usually warm and friendly, and Valerie was shaken by the difference in her manner. Was it an omen of what was to come when they were finally summoned into Nick Caspian's office?

Huskily, she asked Hazel, 'How's Piet?' hoping to coax a real smile out of her.

Hazel gave her an odd look, said in an offhand way, 'He's fine, thanks,' and did not smile as she said it. She got up and went over to file a letter in one of the drawers of a cabinet against the wall, and Valerie bit her lip. Well, mentioning Piet hadn't helped, had it? In fact, she felt it had been a mistake. This must be even more serious than she had feared. What did Hazel know that she didn't? Maybe she was about to get the sack?

Of course, it could be that she had made a psychological mistake in mentioning Piet. Hazel could be depressed because she so rarely saw her husband. After all, they were forced at the moment to live in different countries! That could not be much fun for a newly married couple, even though they saw each other most weekends.

Hazel hadn't quite been married for two months yet, to Piet van Leyden, a Dutch architect who had worked for Caspian International for years. Hazel had gone on working in London, for Nick, since she came back from the honeymoon. She was highly paid, and probably wouldn't get another job as good as the one she had, but it did mean she and Piet had had to live apart since their wedding.

Piet was living in Holland, finishing a major job in Utrecht, where Caspian International were building a massive printing works which would serve all the various national newspapers in the group. Piet was chief architect to the Caspian group in Europe, he moved around from country to country as his work dictated, and hadn't yet settled down anywhere.

He did have family in Holland, of course—his parents, now retired and living quietly in the country, and his sister, Lilli, who lived in the little town of Middleburg, near Flushing, with her husband, Dr Hans Kerk, and their two children, Karel and Karen. Valerie remembered Piet's family, from the wedding. She had envied Hazel; it had been a wonderfully romantic wedding.

It must have been something of an anticlimax after the ceremony to come back to everyday life in the office—perhaps that explained Hazel's mood?

Suddenly, Valerie heard deep male voices raised behind the door to Nick Caspian's office, and felt the palms of her hands start to sweat. What were they saying?

The door from the corridor opened, making her jump and look round, her eyes wide and startled, especially as she recognised the new arrival.

It was the girl she had seen with Gilbey Collingwood earlier, in the riverside gardens. She quickly walked over to Hazel's desk and put a large blue folder on it.

'The documents Mr Caspian wanted!'

'Oh, thanks, Sophie,' Hazel answered in an absent voice, and the other girl nodded and left again, briefly glancing at the other two women as she walked past them, her slender body very graceful in the flowing lines of the poppy-printed dress.

Valerie couldn't stand it, she had to know. 'Who was that?' she asked Hazel, who looked at her in surprise.

'Sophie Watson.'

'Where does she work?'

'She's a secretary in the legal department.'

'I thought I'd seen her before!' Valerie thought aloud.

'I expect you have,' said Hazel, without real interest.

Valerie frequently had to visit the legal department's office on this floor, to get clearance on some story she was writing. She must often have seen Sophie Watson, without the other girl really impinging on her attention.

Hazel got up and went into Nick Caspian's office, taking the blue folder with her. Colette gave Valerie a wry sideways glance.

'Don't look so nervous. They won't eat you.'

'Sure?' Valerie muttered and Colette laughed.

'Look, things aren't as black as all that. The lawyers gave you the go-ahead on publishing, which is a big plus in your favour, and the tape of the interview is another point for you. If Molly Green lied they can't blame you. Her evidence was pretty convincing, and after seeing those photos I don't see how Mac Cameron can win a case against us.'

Valerie gave Colette a grateful look. 'Do you really think so? I hope you're right, and thanks for backing me up, I really appreciate it.'

'I'm features page editor,' Colette said coolly. 'I'm responsible for what goes into my page, whoever wrote it.'

Hazel returned and held the door open for them. 'Mr Caspian will see you now.'

Valerie's heart leapt into her mouth. She followed Colette into the other room, which at first glance seemed full of men. It was the one behind the desk who mattered, though. However many other men were around, Nick Caspian always seemed to compel every eye; he had a presence which was hard to ignore.

He wasn't handsome, he was far too tough for that— a man with a Mediterranean colouring, black hair, a tanned olive skin, he had a strongly chiselled face, a lean, wiry, energetic body and a personality that matched it.

He dominated any room he entered, and Valerie sensed that once he made up his mind he was immovable.

She wouldn't like to find herself on the other side of any war he was waging.

Two chairs had been placed for them, in front of his large leather-covered desk. He gestured, his grey eyes hard. 'Please sit down, Miss Knight, Miss Tse.'

They obeyed; Valerie shot a hurried glanced around the room and suddenly realised that there was one other woman present. Gina Tyrrell sat by the window, her russet hair given a golden gleam by the late afternoon sunlight. As Valerie met her eyes, Gina gave her a friendly smile, and Valerie smiled quickly back, glad Gina was there. It made her feel that at least one person present would be sympathetic to her, and Gina had a lot of influence.

Before Nick Caspian had managed to absorb the *Sentinel* into his Europe-wide empire, the newspaper had been owned by the Tyrrell family for generations. The last owner, Sir George Tyrrell, had dreamed of moving from Fleet Street to a lower-rated site with more space, down by the riverside, but buying the Barbary Wharf site and then building the huge complex had meant borrowing enormous sums of money. When interest rates began to rise Sir George had found himself in serious difficulties, financially, which was when Nick Caspian began to take an interest.

There had been a struggle between the two men which had ended in Sir George being forced to make a deal with Nick Caspian. Shortly afterwards, the old man had died, leaving his estate entirely to Gina, the widow of his grandson, James. Gina had married into the Tyrrell family when she was very young, and been widowed only a couple of years later.

Having lost her own parents, she had continued to live with Sir George, who had been even more devastated by his grandson's death than Gina had been. The old man had needed all the comfort Gina could give him, and she had been comforted by knowing how much he needed her. Over the years they had grown closer and closer, and Sir George's death had been a bitter shock to her.

Everyone on the *Sentinel* knew Gina believed Nick Caspian was to blame for that death. Sir George had died at a dinner given for the staff just before the big move from Fleet Street to Barbary Wharf. Most people had heard rumours and gossip about what happened, but nobody knew for sure exactly what had caused the old man's heart attack. The only thing people knew for certain was that there had been a bitter outburst from Gina Tyrrell, in public, the night Sir George died; many people had actually overheard what she said.

Although since then she had continued to work very closely with Nick Caspian, and was on the board of directors, it was well known that Gina often clashed with Nick, and opposed his decisions. Gossip and rumour travelled fast at Barbary Wharf, often getting magnified in the process, but some whispers were true enough, and Valerie had often seen Gina and Nick Caspian together. She knew there was a deep-seated enmity between them.

'This is only a preliminary meeting, Miss Knight,' Nick Caspian said quietly. 'Do you know our lawyers, Guy Faulkner, and Henry Sandel?'

Valerie glanced at the two men on his right, who rose to shake her hand. The older of the two was Henry Sandel; he was balding, short, with a bland, pale, egg-shaped face. She had met him on a number of earlier occasions and she knew that his expression never seemed to change; he always seemed politely neutral.

The younger man, Guy Faulkner, was much closer to her own age. He was around six feet, had a thin, clever face and blue eyes, smooth, darkish hair. He had taken his law degree rather later than usual, having taken an arts degree and became a journalist only to decide he preferred the law. Because of his background he was something of an expert on newspaper litigation.

'Yes, it was Mr Faulkner who gave me the clearance on the Molly Green interview,' she said, and Guy Faulkner gave her a wry look.

'Have you brought with you the tape and notebook in which you recorded the interview with Molly Green, Miss Knight?' he asked.

'Yes,' Valerie said, placing them on the desk. 'And I've got the photographs she gave me.'

Guy Faulkner spread them out in a fan shape, looking down at the almost naked bodies splayed on the deck of the film star's luxury yacht.

Cameron's losing his hair,' he said with a twist of the lips. 'Look, you can see it quite clearly in this picture. Did we use that one? Maybe that's why he's threatening to sue!'

Henry Sandel watched, his eyes shrewd. 'Before we hear the tape or look at the notebook, I want you to tell me precisely what you recall of that interview, especially with regard to the girl herself. What did you really make of her, Miss Knight? Did you believe her to be entirely truthful? Did you have any doubts about her at all?' He gave her a smooth smile. 'And don't be nervous—you aren't on trial here.'

Valerie did not believe him.

CHAPTER TWO

WHEN the conference broke up several hours later Valerie walked out looking almost shell-shocked, her face drained of colour and her eyes dark with weariness.

Gina Tyrrell looked after her, sighing. 'Poor girl. This is very bad luck for her.'

'Maybe it will teach her a few useful lessons!' Nick bit out without much sympathy.

Gina turned on him. 'That's not fair! You can't say she didn't follow procedure! She taped the interview, and made her own notes at the same time, and those photos made the story look very authentic.' She stood up, her hair the colour of maple leaves in autumn, a gleaming reddish gold, the face beneath it flushed with anger. Nobody made her as furious as Nick could do!

'Don't tell me what I can or can't say!' Nick reacted with temper, too. It had been a difficult day, this was not the only legal threat on his horizon, and he was in no mood to have a woman push him around, especially Gina.

Every time he turned around lately she seemed to be there, blocking him, arguing with him, opposing him in everything he tried to do. He was used to getting his own way, especially with women, and this woman in particular had the power to get right under his skin. She was winning some of their contests, and he was afraid other people had begun to notice.

Tactfully, the editor, Fabien Arnaud, intervened. 'I suspect it was because other papers have followed up on our story by pestering Mac Cameron that he's angry

enough to threaten a lawsuit! I heard over lunch that
every tabloid in town was sending reporters looking for
a different angle, and most of them are going for Mac,
not Molly Green.'

'Valerie said she was in the country, and her mother
wouldn't give out her address!' reminded Guy Faulkner,
the younger lawyer.

The other men gave him amused grins. 'I noticed you
fancied her,' Fabien teased.

Guy looked bland and didn't admit or deny it. Gina
gave him a curious look. He had seemed interested in
Valerie, but then men usually were! She was what men
thought women should look like—blonde, curvy, with
big blue-violet eyes! Gina didn't know Guy Faulkner very
well and wasn't sure what she thought of him, but,
whether he really fancied Valerie or not, one thing was
certain. He was a good lawyer; he gave nothing away.

'I wonder when Molly Green left town,' he murmured, his eyes narrowed and thoughtful. 'Before Valerie
broke the story, or afterwards?'

They all stared at him. Nick tapped his fingers on the
leather top of the desk behind which he sat. It had once
belonged to his father, Zachariah Caspian, whose
portrait hung on the wall behind him. Every time Gina
saw that painting she was reminded of Sir George Tyrrell,
whose picture should hang there, and of the bitterness
she still felt towards Nick. Yet at the same time she
couldn't help wondering about the man who had founded
the Caspian empire and left it all to his son when he
died. Zachariah Caspian had an interesting face. Nick
had inherited something of his father's looks—or was it
more that he had inherited his father's nature and it
showed in both their faces? Tough, acquisitive, determined—they were not easy men to know or like.

'You suspect Molly told Valerie Knight a tissue of lies then skipped town?' Nick bit out now and Guy Faulkner shrugged.

'Maybe. Or she may have told Valerie the truth, then panicked and run. Whichever it is, she must be found and we must go over her with a fine-tooth comb and make sure we're getting the truth, the whole truth and nothing but the truth, this time.'

'Valerie Knight should have made sure of that the first time!' Nick muttered, scowling. 'If she costs us a fortune in legal fees, she'll be out on her ear!'

Angrily, Gina said, 'You're more to blame than Valerie! You're the one who talks about giving the paper teeth, daring to print what other papers won't touch, but at the first hint of any trouble, you lose your nerve! If you can't stand the heat, stay out of the kitchen!'

Everyone else in the room suddenly turned into little wooden statues, not hearing or seeing anything.

Nick got to his feet, breathing so angrily they could all hear him, and glared down at her, teeth tight. 'You have never wanted me to modernise the *Sentinel*, have you?'

'No, I haven't. You can call it modernising but I call it wanton destruction of a great newspaper!'

'You've done everything you could think of to stop me, in fact!'

'I certainly have—I only wish I'd succeeded!'

'Right,' he bit out. 'And only last week you said that reporters like Valerie Knight had no place on the *Sentinel*!'

'And she doesn't! All these cheap gossip items, the invasions of privacy, the sneering and innuendo, are against everything the *Sentinel* once stood for! I know Valerie's popular, she sells papers, the readers like her stuff, but I would rather she didn't work on the *Sentinel*.'

'Then why are you taking her side now,' roared Nick, 'unless to annoy me!'

'Sir George believed in being loyal to the people who worked for him,' she calmly told him.

'Sir George!' he snarled. 'I might have known! I knew his name would come up sooner or later. Is he going to haunt me for the rest of my life?'

The amusement left Gina's eyes. 'I hope so,' she said, and turned round to walk away, towards the door.

'Don't walk out on me when I'm talking to you!' Nick shouted after her. 'I wanted to discuss something else, something important.'

'Send me a memo.' Gina opened the door and Nick came after her, leaving the others in his office.

'We're leaving for California on Thursday next, remember!'

'I have important appointments all next week,' she said, her voice like the wind from the Steppes; icy and devastating.

There was a silence, and Nick looked down at her with rage in his grey eyes. 'You can't back out now! You knew I'd made arrangements for you, too. You must come. What am I to say to my mother?'

'Your mother?' Gina repeated, taken aback. He had mentioned that his mother lived in San Francisco, but the trip to California was supposed to be purely business, so she had assumed that her meeting with Mrs Caspian would be extremely brief.

He glowered, his brows heavy. 'I told her you were coming, and she invited you to stay with her. What excuse am I supposed to give her if you don't turn up?'

Gina was astonished. He could not be serious! His mother had never met her, probably didn't even know who she was! Why should she care whether or not Gina arrived with the rest of the party going out to California to investigate the possibility of Caspian International moving into the American market?

'I'm sure she won't even notice!' she said, and at that moment Hazel came towards them with a sheaf of papers for Nick to sign, and he had to let go of Gina's shoulder. She walked away without a backward look and heard the office door close a moment later, but she couldn't get his expression out of her mind while she was taking the lift down to the car park and getting into her car. Why was he so insistent on taking her to California? She couldn't believe that it really was his mother's reaction he was worried about. Nick always had an ulterior motive, if not two, for everything he did. So why did he want her to go on this trip? What was Nick really up to?

She didn't trust him, not an inch. He was devious, ruthless, a man determined always to be the winner at everything he did. That was how he saw life—as a race to be run, a fight to be fought—and he believed that 'to the victor...the spoils'.

Gina had no intention of ending up as the spoils Nick Caspian claimed as his prize for victory.

Ever since he bought the only other flat on the penthouse floor of her apartment block she had felt the net closing in around her. She saw Nick every day in the office, now he was living right next door, and although she kept refusing all his social invitations and tried to keep her private life separate from her working day Nick somehow kept intruding. He was always offering her lifts to work, calling at her flat on the pretence of needing information that couldn't wait, asking her to join him and other directors in his flat for drinks.

Gina often wanted to smack him, but she did the next best thing. She showed him a cool, remote face and kept him at arm's length, whatever approach he made.

As she drove along beside the river it began to rain, a heavy, drenching downpour which made passers-by who had been languidly wandering along in the humid evening air start to run towards shop doorways and Underground stations.

Gina looked up at the cloudy sky and grimaced. She had been looking forward to a relaxing weekend in the country, but if it didn't stop raining by tomorrow morning she would cancel her plans to stay at the little country pub in Sussex which ran a painting course for beginners. Of course, they could no doubt stay indoors and paint in a studio, but that wouldn't be the same, she decided. What had attracted her was the idea of going out and painting in the open air, seeing something of the local countryside as well as learning a new skill. She could always go some other time.

Instead, on Saturday, she would go to Selfridges, buy a tape of that new album she wanted, check out the latest fashion they had in the store, have a light lunch in their restaurant, and in the evening go to the theatre. Gina didn't like anything too heavy. She liked to be entertained when she went out for the evening, and she particularly liked musical comedy.

When she got home she made herself a cup of coffee, curled up on her couch with that morning's copy of the *Sentinel* and skated her eye down the theatre list. She had been to most of the good musicals, but there was a new one in the Strand which she hadn't yet seen, and it had had good reviews.

She put a coral-pink fingertip on the item, and then her green eyes opened wider. Of course! She had forgotten! Mac Cameron was playing the lead in the show, although only for a six-week run. No doubt he had another film role lined up after that, but having him as their star had helped to get the new musical off with a bang. The Press had been wild with enthusiasm.

Gina rang the box office at once, half expecting to be told there were no tickets left, but she was lucky. There had been one ticket returned a few minutes before she rang, the box office girl told her. It was in the front row of the stalls. Gina took it.

It was already raining when Valerie Knight left Barbary Wharf. She had come to work by bus and groaned as she halted in the doorway, seeing a long queue at the bus stop in Silver Street. She hadn't expected the weather to change so abruptly and wasn't wearing a coat.

Maybe she should walk round to the taxi rank? But in this weather she was not likely to find any taxis waiting; others would have had the same idea.

A car emerged from the underground car park below Barbary Wharf and turned into North Street, close to the exit where Valerie was sheltering. It slowly drove towards her and as it drew level she noticed it, and peered hopefully through the driving rain. If she knew the driver she might get a lift. But who did she know who drove a dark red Jaguar?

The window wound down electronically, the door was pushed open and Valerie ran forward, feeling the wind tugging at her expensive hairstyle, the rain soaking into her thin dress.

She saw Gilbey Collingwood's face behind the wheel just before she got into the car and stopped, staring at him.

'Any port in a storm!' he mocked and she almost turned away, but he was right. She really had no option. Just standing here for a minute was turning her into a drowned mouse.

She scrambled into the front seat and slammed the door shut. 'Thanks!' she said stiffly.

'My pleasure,' he drawled and a little shiver ran down her back. She didn't like the way he had said that.

He hadn't driven on again; instead he shifted in his seat, stretching a long arm backwards, and Valerie tensed, giving him a wary look. What was he doing? Maybe this was a serious mistake. It might be wiser to get out again now.

Then he produced a box of paper tissues from the back seat and offered it to her. 'Here, mop up with these!'

She took the box and Gib drove on into the slashing spears of rain while Valerie began carefully drying her face. She hoped her mascara hadn't run. When she was more or less dry she got out her powder compact and examined herself.

'You look as gorgeous as usual, don't worry,' Gib said without looking, his eyes on the wet road ahead.

Valerie ignored him and set about repairing the ravages of the weather.

As always in London on rainy days, there seemed far more traffic than usual and people on the pavements had a desperate air, knowing there would be no taxis, the buses would be full, the underground trains crowded. On days like this people wondered why they lived and worked in this crazy city and dreamt of getting out of it all, moving into the tranquil countryside, not having to make these long journeys every day.

Her lipstick needed renewing, her nose was shiny, her blonde hair sparkled with dewdrops of rain. She slowly dealt with all that, wishing she were not so conscious of Gib's lean body in the car beside her. Driving with him in this small space, with the rain somehow turning the car into an island in the centre of this river of traffic, was a faintly disturbing experience. She had kept him at arm's length for so long that being alone with him now made her as tense as if he was a real threat to her, which was ridiculous, of course. She could deal with any man, and she certainly wasn't scared of Gilbey Collingwood! And anyway, rationally, she knew he wasn't the type to turn nasty. So why was her heart beating in that irregular way, and why were her nerves jumping?

'Isn't this where you live?' Gib said, slowing, and she looked out, startled to have arrived so quickly.

'Yes, thanks,' she said in relief, getting ready to leap out of the car.

'Hang on, I've got an umbrella.' Gib reached over into the back of the car again, found the umbrella and got out before she could stop him. She opened her door but as she clambered out she found Gib towering over her, the umbrella held over her head. 'Stand still!' he commanded as she began to move, and, startled, she froze instinctively. Gib leaned down and locked the car.

'OK,' he said, took her elbow and hurried her up the paved path to the entrance to the recently built block of flats. Valerie had only moved in there that summer, having bought a lease on a one-bedroom flat.

Suddenly a thought occurred to her. How had Gilbey Collingwood known where she lived? He hadn't asked her. He had driven straight here, he had known exactly where he was going! The realisation alarmed her.

Once they were inside the building, out of the rain, she pulled her arm out of his grip and gave him a cold, polite smile.

'Thanks for the lift. Goodnight.'

Before he could react she turned away and walked over to the stairs. Her flat was on the first floor so she didn't bother to take the lift, just ran hurriedly up the short flight of stairs.

On the landing she paused to look back, but there was no sign of Gib. The hall was empty. He had accepted his dismissal and gone. Well, thank heavens for that! she told herself, but didn't feel any happier. In fact, her mood was depressed as she slid her key into her flat front door. Nothing to do with Gilbey Collingwood, of course—it was just that she had had a very bad day, what with the news of Esteban getting engaged to someone else, and the threatened law suit by Mac Cameron.

She walked into the small hallway of her flat but as she turned to close the door she found herself confronting Gib.

'What...' she stammered, too startled to think quickly, and he walked past her into her sitting-room while she was still adjusting to the sight of him.

Valerie felt adrenalin pump into her veins; she was flushed and breathless with temper as she pursued him. 'What are you doing? I didn't invite you up here!'

'No, you didn't, did you? Not very polite of you, after I'd rescued you from imminent drowning and driven you all the way home!' he told her reproachfully, picking up one of the silver-framed photographs on a table. 'Are these your parents?'

'Yes,' she said crossly, knowing that if anyone else had given her a lift from work she would have automatically invited them in for a drink.

'I can see a family resemblance. You take after your mother, don't you?' Before she could answer, he added, 'Aren't you going to offer me a cup of coffee, at least?'

'Very well, I'll make some coffee,' Valerie said through her teeth.

'How gracious!' he mocked, following her into her tiny kitchenette and staring around him curiously. 'There isn't room to swing a cat!'

'I haven't got one to swing.'

'Then I won't have to report you for cruelty to animals!'

Valerie ignored that. She was in no mood for one of his jokes. The trouble with Gilbey Collingwood was his sense of humour, he didn't take anything seriously, which was one reason why she couldn't take him seriously. Why should she?

She was making instant coffee in mugs—she wasn't wasting time making real coffee for him—and she didn't look round although she was very aware of him prowling around, opening the door of her tiny fridge, inspecting the meagre contents, which she knew by heart. They were all left-overs; a few scraps of smoked salmon, some cottage cheese, a slice of melon and a wedge of iceberg lettuce. She would make a light supper later from a mixture of all four, although she wasn't excited by the prospect.

'Is that all you have to eat in the place?' demanded Gib, closing the fridge door again.

'Yes.' Her tone dared him to comment. 'Your coffee is ready.' Valerie carried the tray through to the sitting-room with him right behind her, almost breathing down her neck. She felt more like chucking the coffee at him instead of handing it over with a polite smile. Discretion triumphed. 'Here you are,' she said, sweet as saccharin, then sat down with her own coffee in an isolated chair by the window, leaving him to sit down on the couch or another chair even further away.

To her fury, he put his coffee down on the mantel-piece and moved his chair nearer to hers, so that they almost touched, then he picked up his mug again and sat down, his sideways glance gleaming with amusement at her look of suppressed rage.

Just as she was about to order him out of her flat his face changed, the smile went and he looked seriously at her.

'I was sorry to hear about this threatened lawsuit. What do the legal people say? Are they worried?'

She sobered too, nodding. 'I spent all afternoon talking to them.' Then she frowned. 'How did you hear about it? It's supposed to be a deadly secret for the moment.'

'I know someone in the legal department.'

Valerie remembered then. 'Sophie!' she muttered, and Gib gave her a surprised look.

'That's right. How do you know that?'

Valerie didn't tell him. 'She's supposed to be discreet, you know,' was all she said, in a tart voice. 'She isn't supposed to gossip about what she hears to all her menfriends.'

He frowned. 'I'm sure she doesn't gossip about her work at all!'

'Oh, only to you?' Valerie knew she sounded acid, but it wasn't deliberate, it just kept coming out that way. Mind you, she was in the right and Gib knew it. Sophie was in a very privileged position, she must hear confidential information every day and there was no doubt that she would lose her job if anyone discovered that she was gossiping. The legal department couldn't afford to have someone working for them who leaked secrets.

Gib hesitated, his brows together in a black frown. Then he said curtly, 'She knows I know you.'

'All the more reason why she shouldn't have told you!'

His mouth was a hard line, his usually smiling eyes dark and fierce. 'We're at it again, aren't we?' he burst out suddenly. 'Sooner or later we end up fighting like cat and dog—and I know damn well it isn't me who provokes these rows. It's always you. You have the personality of a porcupine. Whichever way I approach you

I end up with a handful of prickles. What is it about this time? A friend of mine happens to mention that you're in trouble, and she had the best of intentions; Sophie is a good kid. Unlike you, she doesn't have a bad temper or a suspicious mind. She was being kind.'

I bet, thought Valerie, her ears buzzing from the grating of his angry voice. I'm sure dear little Sophie had the best of motives for telling him that I might be about the lose my job. It must have been a sad shock for her to realise that I could soon be out of the firm, off the newspaper, out of her way, leaving Gib entirely to her. Obviously, she could hardly wait, so she didn't. She told him the skids were under me and I was probably under notice already.

'She still shouldn't have told you!' was all she said, though.

There was a little silence, then Gib asked brusquely, 'You aren't going to mention this to anyone, are you? With your own job under threat, surely you wouldn't want to be the cause of Sophie losing her job?'

He was obviously very concerned over Sophie. Valerie looked away, her face blank. Odd to think of the light-hearted, teasing Gib being that serious over anyone!

He was right, though. She certainly wouldn't want to be the cause of the other girl losing her job, even if Sophie didn't seem to care that much about it or she surely wouldn't risk losing it.

'No, I won't say a word, but I think you had better warn her that if Nick Caspian hears she's given to gossiping he'll come down on her like a ton of bricks.'

Gib nodded. 'I'm sure you're right. He's a tough boss if you make a mistake.' There was a pause, then drily, 'Did he come down on you like a ton of bricks?'

'No, he was quite fair,' Valerie said, faintly surprised herself. 'Tough, but fair-minded. He asked some penetrating questions, nothing gets by him, but he gave me a chance to put my side of the story, and he listened.'

'I read the interview with that girl. She sounded naïve and rather sweet—do you still believe her story, or does it look as if she was lying?'

Valerie gave him a straight look, her blue eyes sharp. 'I've been warned not to talk about the case. Sorry.'

Gib nodded unsmilingly. 'I understand. Quite right. I shouldn't have asked. But if there is ever any way I can help, anything I can do, you only have to ask.'

'Thank you,' she said, startled, looking down, rather pink, and another silence fell between them, but with a different feel to it this time, an intangible atmosphere Valerie couldn't quite define. She remembered abruptly that moment in the car in the rainy street when she had felt she was on an island with Gib, isolated, intimately alone. That was how it felt now.

He suddenly got to his feet. 'Now, how about dinner? You can't really want to eat that odd jumble of stuff in your fridge. Why don't we go out to eat a real meal somewhere? I know a very good Italian restaurant not far from here.'

She was flushed and stammering. 'No, I...thank you but...really, I can't. My diet...Italian food is so fattening.'

'Fish isn't,' he said. 'They do wonderful trout grilled with almonds—that isn't fattening, and you can start with melon and parma ham, hardly any calories at all.'

She looked desperately at the rain-streaked windows. 'Going out in this terrible weather would be crazy.'

'I have my umbrella and my car is parked right outside.' He took her arm. 'Come on, stop arguing.'

'But...'

'No buts,' he firmly told her. 'We have a lot to talk about.'

Valerie gave him a wary look. 'What?'

'I'll tell you my life story,' he promised with a return of the familiar mockery. 'And you can tell me yours.'

'There's nothing to tell!' she said, not sure whether to laugh or be irritated by that teasing note in his voice.

'I shall be fascinated by every word,' he drawled, and she laughed, a little impatiently.

'You think you're so funny, don't you?'

'You obviously don't!' he said with a mock-mournful look, and then he was whisking her out of the flat and downstairs out into the rain, his umbrella held over her head until they reached his car.

The drive to the Italian restaurant was brief, a matter of two blocks, and they were able to park quite nearby.

'What if they don't have a table free?' Valerie asked as they ran through the rain, under Gib's umbrella.

'They will!' he assured her.

'It *is* Friday night, they may be full!'

He ushered her through the door into the crowded, noisy restaurant and the waiter came up to them, grinning at Gib.

'You're late, but I kept your table, as I know you!'

Valerie gave Gib a sharp, accusing look, but he didn't look her way, he just smiled sunnily at the waiter.

'Thanks, Rico. I got held up.' Only then did he slide a brief glance at Valerie, and Rico laughed.

'Well, she was worth waiting for! Welcome to Rico's, *signorina*. I hope we are going to see you many times in the future.' His eyes admired her blonde hair, her deep violet-blue eyes, her sexy figure, and Valerie stiffened. She was used to getting that sort of look, and she liked knowing she looked good, but at times it made her edgy. Every man seemed to feel he could flirt with her, make personal remarks, stare openly, just because of the way she looked. If she had been plain they wouldn't react like that; they would probably treat her with more respect!

She sensed Gib watching her and shot him a look. He was frowning. Suddenly, he put an arm around her. 'Have I got my usual table, Rico?' he asked in an offhand way.

The waiter's manner subtly changed, picking up Gib's silent signal. 'Of course,' he said, gesturing towards the far end of the room. 'You know your way. Shall I bring the wine or do you want an aperitif first?'

'The wine, thanks, Rico,' Gib said, steering Valerie through the closely set tables.

'Maybe I wanted an aperitif,' she muttered, resenting his high-handed manner and the possessive arm clamped round her waist. The only reason she didn't slap it away was because she knew it was there to impress on Rico the fact that she was there with Gib and that the waiter should keep his distance.

'Did you?' Gib challenged, his face impatient.

'No, but——'

'Then what are you complaining about?'

'About not being given the choice!' she snapped as they reached a table in the furthest corner.

Gib pulled out a chair and held it for her. 'I'll remember to ask next time,' he promised solemnly, but she caught the glimmer of mockery in his hazel eyes and knew he was secretly laughing at her.

'When did you book this table?' she asked him and he shrugged.

'I have a standard booking every Friday evening.'

'And every week there's a different girl?' she sarcastically murmured, and he gave her one of those teasing looks.

'I can't imagine why you say that!'

She laughed without humour. 'Of course not! So, what happened to the girl who should be here instead of me? Did she dump you, or did she get dumped?'

'I hadn't made a date with anyone. I meant to ring up and cancel my table; I often do that and Rico doesn't mind because on Fridays he is always busy.

She didn't believe him. Gilbey Collingwood, without a date, on a Friday evening? Did he think she was unaware of his reputation?

She had known a whole string of girls who had dated Gib over the past months. They were always pretty, usually light-hearted; he seemed to go for that type. He didn't like intense, emotional girls, no doubt because they made too much fuss when he ended the affair. Gib's attention span wasn't long enough; he took a girl out once, maybe twice, and then moved on, leaving them to do the same. She had to admit that his ex-girlfriends never seemed to harbour a grudge, or end up with broken hearts. In fact, she often saw him joking with one or other of them, as if they were good friends, and maybe they were.

'Don't tell me it was Sophie!' she said and got a quick, amused look that time.

'OK, I won't.'

Had it been Sophie he intended to bring here this evening? Valerie felt no triumph at the thought that he might have preferred her company to that of the other girl. Next time it might be the other way around! Men like Gib were unpredictable, and Valerie did not like unpredictability. She liked life stable and familiar and safe.

Rico arrived with the wine and Gib courteously asked her, 'Is this wine OK with you, or would you rather look at the wine list and choose something else?'

She caught Rico's look of startled surprise and hid a smile, inspecting the label on the bottle with a serious air.

She was no expert on wines, she only drank them to be polite, and at home never drank anything but mineral water or fruit juice, but she wasn't going to let either man guess that.

'Fine with me,' she said, shrugging, and picked up the menu Rico had placed on the table and began studying that. Most of the dishes sounded very fattening, but she had to agree with what Gib had told her—the melon and parma ham, followed by trout, with a salad, sounded her best choice.

Gib chose to start with aubergine baked with mozzarella cheese and tomato sauce, and for his main course asked for a *fritto misto*, a deep-fried mixture of squid, prawns, scallops, and white fish served with fresh vegetables.

'Easy to see you aren't dieting,' Valerie said drily after Rico had taken their order and left.

'I exercise for several hours a day, and I rarely eat this well,' Gib told her with a grin. 'Usually I skip breakfast, too, except for orange juice and a coffee. My weight hasn't varied much in years.'

She considered him. He had a very good, athletic figure, a long, slim, muscled body—what did he look like without all those clothes on? she wondered, then felt heat stealing into her face at the idea.

Startled, she guiltily looked up and found herself looking into his quizzical eyes.

Gib said softly, 'You're unnervingly quiet. What are you thinking about?'

Surely he hadn't guessed? she thought, panic-stricken, but how could he? You couldn't read people's thoughts from their faces. Could you?

'About dieting,' she said. 'You're so lucky, not having to bother. I put on a pound if I so much as look at a potato.'

She wished she hadn't let him stampede her into having dinner with him. She had managed to lock Gilbey Collingwood out of her head so far. She shouldn't have weakened. Look what she was thinking about now!

Come to that, look at the conversation they were having! He had managed to sneak up on her somehow, without her noticing. Only a week ago she had been walking away every time he came within a foot of her, and now here she was, having dinner with him, wondering what he looked like naked, and lying to him in case he guessed!

Rico appeared with their first course, and Valerie averted her eyes from Gib's delicous-looking aubergine dish.

'What made you switch from working in the City to journalism?' she asked, instead.

'I was bored with high finance,' confessed Gib. 'I earned a lot of money, but the lifestyle was dreary and exhausting. I know people believe that anyone who works in the City gets a huge salary and only has to work a few hours a day, but that's a myth. The truth is, if you want to keep your job and hope for promotion, you have to get there by eight in the morning, and often work until eight at night. The higher you climb, the harder you have to work, until you get right to the top and then, I suppose, you can relax, go off and play golf, take three-hour lunch breaks.' He grimaced at her. 'I wasn't prepared to spend my life working like a donkey on a treadmill, so I got out.'

'I don't blame you,' she said between mouthfuls of melon. 'It sounds ghastly.'

'Some people like the life, it suits them. It didn't suit me.'

'How did you get the job you're doing now, though, if you have no background in journalism?'

'By stealth,' he said, grinning. 'I was lucky enough to spot a job going in accounting, on the *Sentinel*, in the days when the Tyrrell's still owned the paper. I got that job, and began looking about me, considering my next move. I could see it wasn't going to be easy to get what I wanted; it would take a lot of time and patience, because I was switching from one type of expertise to another, and journalists operate a sort of closed shop. I'd had no journalistic training, so I started going to night school and learning about writing. Meanwhile, I made friends with everyone on the business news section of the paper, I started slipping in titbits of gossip I'd picked up, then longer pieces, articles on specialist subjects, until I'd built up a reputation, and eventually I managed to get taken on there.'

Valerie looked at him narrowly. His account of how he had got his job on the *Sentinel* told her far more about Gilbey Collingwood than he would probably want her to know.

He was an impressive operator, one had to admit that. When he wanted something, there were no limits to his patience and determination, no lengths to which he would not go. He had said so himself. Oh, he had been talking about his professional career, but Valerie was thinking more about his private life.

Gib had made no secret of the fact that he wanted her, and he had been chasing her for a very long time, doggedly, unswervingly, with a terrifying patience. He had never got anywhere, because he was married, and she didn't go out with married men, even if they swore they were getting a divorce.

In fact, she didn't go out with divorced men, either, because somehow she didn't trust a man who hadn't managed to make his first marriage work.

So why was she here with Gib tonight, in spite of that? Valerie didn't know. She hadn't meant to go out with Gib. It had just happened. He had sneaked up on her and talked her out of her flat and out to dinner with him. Gilbey Collingwood was a very persuasive man.

But his relationships never lasted. His marriage certainly hadn't—although there was no evidence as to whose fault that was. Since his wife and he had parted, however, he had dated a lot of girls, once or at most twice and then never again. That was fact. Valerie knew that from watching him over the past year, seeing him with one girl then another, so briefly that their faces blurred in her mind.

She didn't know how far his relationship with these girls had ever gone. Maybe he just took them out, kissed them goodnight and went home. But maybe he didn't. Maybe he slept with them before he said goodbye and vanished like the Wicked Fairy in a puff of smoke.

Whatever the pattern, Valerie didn't intend to become part of it. She wasn't sleeping with Gib and being dropped next day. She had discovered now the technique he used to get what he wanted—water dropping on a stone, you could call it. Sooner or later, he believed, he would be successful. Well, he was wrong. She had made a mistake in coming out to dinner with him, but she wouldn't make the same mistake again. This time the dumping was being done by the girl, not Gib.

CHAPTER THREE

ON SATURDAY morning, the torrential rain continued and the wind whipped the Thames into a boiling cauldron. Gina got up at seven, heavy-eyed and yawning, just to check on the weather, drew back her curtains and looked out, then stumbled back to bed. No, she certainly was not driving into the country to learn painting today!

When she got up again at around ten o'clock it was still raining, but by the time she had drunk a cup of coffee and eaten an apple there were patches of blue sky between heavy showers. At eleven-thirty she took a taxi to the West End of London, to Oxford Street, to check out the latest brightly coloured fun tights which had just come into the shops. They were already being worn by some girls on the newspaper, but Gina hadn't got the nerve to go into the office wearing bold yellow or acid-green tights. She might wear them to a casual party, though, in the right shade, so she went from shop to shop looking at the range of colours.

She was in Debenham's when she walked into Valerie Knight, who was also examining fun tights.

'Oh, hello!' they said together, then laughed.

'I thought you were going away for the weekend!' Valerie said.

'I was,' admitted Gina, explaining why she hadn't gone.

'Oh, you shouldn't have let the weather stop you. It's just as much fun painting indoors as out.'

'Do you paint?'

'Well, I was quite good when I was at school and I've often meant to take it more seriously, but you know what this job is like. There's never any time for anything else. But painting is better than going into therapy—and cheaper!'

Gina laughed. 'I'd never thought of it like that!'

Valerie smiled back. 'That's just my opinion, of course! You can get so absorbed in what you're doing that you forget your problems!'

Gina gave her a sympathetic look. 'And at the moment you have got problems, haven't you?'

Valerie flushed to her hairline, looking startled. 'What do you mean?'

'Well...the lawsuit,' said Gina, and Valerie's expression changed.

'Oh! Yes! Of course,' she stammered, rather oddly, Gina felt. What other problems had Valerie got?

Gina watched her curiously. She knew so little about Valerie Knight's private life.

'Do you think Mac Cameron will go through with it?' asked Valerie, and Gina sighed.

'Who knows? People often threaten lawsuits then back out before it ever gets to court. I suppose everything depends on whether or not he really could be the father of that baby. If he knows for certain he isn't, and can prove it, then we could be in trouble.'

Valerie sighed. 'Yes.' But she was grateful to Gina Tyrrell for using the plural, saying 'we' could be in trouble, not dumping the whole problem on to her, so she smiled at her and said impulsively, 'You look terrific in that black coat, very sexy.'

Gina giggled, looking down at the black leather coat. 'It's the only raincoat I've got, actually. I bought it in a rash moment, and I don't wear it often because it's far too short.'

'With your legs, you can afford to wear short clothes,' Valerie told her. 'So, what will you do instead of going away, this weekend?'

'Just relax,' said Gina. 'I don't plan to do anything, actually. I'm rather looking forward to being lazy.' She thought of telling Valerie that she was going to see Mac Cameron at the theatre that evening, then decided that it would not be tactful.

'Good idea, I think I'll do the same!' said Valerie.

'Well, have a good weekend. See you on Monday,' Gina said before she walked away.

She found Valerie something of a puzzle. She had a reputation as something of a honeypot; there were always men around her and she seemed to love their company. She was supposed to be a party animal, loving a good time—yet she was to be seen working in the editorial offices long after others had left, and Fabien Arnaud, the editor of the *Sentinel* had a very high opinion of her.

'She's a hard worker, and has flair, too, a combination that doesn't often happen,' he had told Gina and Nick Caspian yesterday, before Valerie was summoned to their presence.

'Hmm,' Nick had growled, tapping his fingertips on the desk.

Gina hated him in that mood—when he was terse, impatient, offhand.

Fabien hadn't seemed to notice his proprietor's scowl. Calmly, he had gone on, 'I'd be very sorry to lose her. She would be hard to replace. She has a talent for getting people to talk to her, and she writes with sparkle. She can be funny, she can be acid, and she has a real gift for sketching a portrait in a few words. She's very popular.'

'If she skates close to the wind and risks lawsuits, that makes her too expensive for this paper!' Nick had muttered.

'In my experience of her she is careful and sticks to what she can prove,' Fabien had insisted.

Nick had growled, 'But then you always back up your staff, Fabien!'

'Only when I think they deserve it!'

Gina had been delighted with what Fabien said. Usually, she was at loggerheads with the editor. She didn't trust him any more. When he first arrived, he had seemed so charming, but now she thought his was a very surface charm. Like most Swiss, he spoke several languages fluently, but she didn't think he was exactly frank in any of them. He was more of a diplomat than a crusading editor, soothing Nick Caspian down when he flew into one of his towering rages, pouring oil on troubled waters, ready to do whatever Nick wanted. Worst of all, he was the editor now turning the *Sentinel* from a serious newspaper with a high reputation into a brassy, sensation-seeking paper with no scruples and a huge circulation.

She hoped he would go on backing up Valerie Knight, anyway! As she made her way home to a sparing lunch of poached fish and a salad, it occurred to her that she was beginning to like Valerie better than she had until now. Perhaps because she felt sympathy for her? Or because she was seeing a side of Valerie Knight that most people never glimpsed. Just now, she had looked pale, tense, shadows under her blue eyes, as if she hadn't slept all night.

I must ask her out to lunch next week and get to know her better, Gina thought. Getting to know the people who worked for the *Sentinel* had always been part of her job, but it was also something she enjoyed, increasingly so now.

She had no family of her own any more, and with Sir George Tyrrell's death she had lost her closest friend. She still had other friends, of course. Hazel and Piet, Philip Slade, and, most important of all, her old schoolfriend, Roz Amery, who knew more about her than anyone else in the world now.

But Sir George's death had taught her many indelible lessons, and one of them had been that, whether you were happy or sad, up or down, you needed people in your life who cared about you. For months after the traumatic events last winter, she had leant on Roz and Daniel Bruneille, with whom Roz now lived, Hazel and Piet, and Philip Slade. Without them she would have been ten times more desolate. Now Gina made friends whenever she could, wherever she could, and it would be great if she and Valerie could become friends.

Until this week, Gina hadn't liked her much at all. For one things, Valerie was a symbol of what was happening to the *Sentinel*: her features were brash, cheeky, and easy to read. That was why she was so successful.

Also, she had given Gina the impression of being the sort of girl who only liked men, and didn't have any friends among her own sex.

All this was still true, of course, but suddenly the barriers between them were down. Valerie had been friendly this morning, no doubt because she was so worried, and Gina had not only felt sorry for her, she had liked her far better.

But I am sure I was right not to tell her I was going to see Mac Cameron's musical, Gina thought, as she made herself coffee after lunch. Valerie might have thought I was trying to make friends with the enemy!

Although she had a housekeeper who came in every weekday to keep the large penthouse flat immaculate, she liked to look after herself at weekends, unless she had guests. She spent most days surrounded by people, so it was wonderful to be alone for a while, to do as she liked without caring what anyone else thought.

The weather brightened up for a while later in the afternoon, so Gina put on a tracksuit and went out for a run along by the river, watching the gleam of steely light across the water, the skimming gulls chasing each other on the wind. It would soon be autumn, leaves were already turning brown or gold, and she noticed that the horse chestnut tree she was passing had branches heavy with the conkers little London boys hunted for each September, the shiny brown nuts, hidden within prickly green overcoats, which they would harden in vinegar, then thread on to string so that they could do battle with them, the winner being the conker that did not shatter.

Gina smiled to herself as two little boys ran up and excitedly began chucking sticks up into the branches of the tree, hoping to knock down some of the conkers.

The days were getting shorter, too, she realised, as the light began to thicken into dusk, so she turned back. A moment later she saw another jogger loping along towards her, a tall, long-legged figure in a black tracksuit, his dark hair blowing around in the wind. She only needed one look to recognise him, and felt her heart jolt violently.

Then he was level with her and she met his eyes with another shock. Nick was furious, his face hard and tense.

'Are you crazy, running through his area alone, when it's getting dark?' he broke out, halting and catching hold of her arm.

'There's nobody about except a couple of kids!' she protested, and his grey eyes glittered.

'Exactly! If someone attacked you nobody would be around to come to your rescue!'

This was a lonely stretch of road, running beside the river with little traffic on it, she couldn't deny it, but she had never felt worried about running here.

'There are blocks of flats on the other side of the road—someone would be bound to notice if I did get attacked, and ring the police,' she argued. 'And, anyway, it was broad daylight when I set out.'

He looked around, his face coldly ironic. 'It isn't now.'

The light was going fast, the sky clouding over and the wind getting up again. Gina shivered.

'And it's far too cold to go running, anyway!'

'For me, but not for you?' she crossly muttered.

'I only came out because I saw you set off! I couldn't believe my eyes. I didn't think even you would be so foolhardy. The dockland area still isn't a safe place for a woman to be out alone in the evening! So I followed you to make sure you didn't come to any harm.'

'Oh!' she said, startled, flushing, then stammered, 'That was...I'm sure you meant...but there was no need, I was perfectly safe, you see. I often go out for a run.'

'Well, don't do it again!' he snapped. 'Not alone, and only if it's daytime and there are plenty of people around. You don't want to be one of the crime statistics we get from Scotland Yard every week, do you?'

She shivered again, and Nick scowled at her.

'You've probably caught a chill! You must get back at once and take a hot bath.' He set off back towards their apartment block, dragging her along with him.

Gina was too shaken to argue. It moved her to think of Nick getting angry and coming after her when he saw her going out running alone towards evening. Did he really care about her? Her heart turned over, making her even more breathless. He set a pace she found exhausting, although his long legs easily covered the ground. Gina had been running for half an hour; she was tired. With Nick beside her she wasn't going to admit what struggle she was having, though, so she forced herself to go on until they finally got through the front door of the apartment block and into the waiting lift.

Then she reeled against the wall, breathing like old bellows, her leg muscles aching.

Nick watched her with what she sensed to be grim satisfaction. 'You're out of condition!' he informed her. 'I've had a gym installed in the plaza, at Barbary Wharf, you know, you should use it and get yourself into...' He paused. 'Into condition,' he ended, giving her a slanting, mocking smile. 'I was going to say better shape, but with you that doesn't apply. There's nothing at all wrong with your shape.'

She felt his gaze wandering over her figure in the tight-fitting green and white tracksuit and her face burned.

'But you know how sexy you look in that, don't you?' he whispered, and moved closer, his body brushing hers, and her nerves jumped violently.

'Don't!' she snapped, moving away.

'One day, Gina...' he began, his voice hoarse, then he broke off, his teeth coming together. 'Oh, to hell with you, then!'

She tried to ignore him, but her senses were far too conscious of him; she only wished she could read his mind as easily as she picked up his body's signals. At times she was sure he really cared about her. Why else had he followed her just now, to make sure she didn't come to any harm?

But she could never forget the way he had deceived her before, making her believe he loved her and that she could trust him, only to go behind her back, and try to snatch the *Sentinel* in a cold-hearted act of betrayal which had brought on the heart attack that killed Sir George. At that instant Nick had killed her love for him. She had sworn then that she would never forgive him, she would one day manage to make him pay for what he had done—but, ever since, her love and her hate had fought inside her.

She wanted to hate him, but all her energy went into not wanting him, and that was exhausting her. At times she just wanted to go away and forget she had ever met him, forget the *Sentinel* and Sir George and all the conflicts which had been raging inside her for so many months. Only her sense of duty kept her here, and duty was cold comfort for a lonely heart and a frustrated body.

She rigidly stared at the floor, willing the lift to go faster. She had to get away from him or she would go mad.

The lift stopped, and one of them had to insert their key before the lift would go on up to the penthouse floor. Aware of Nick watching her, Gina hurriedly did that, and the lift went on upwards. Then the doors opened, and she shot out and made towards her own front door without looking at him.

Nick was on her heels, like a dog after a rabbit, and she didn't get a chance to get into her flat and slam the door on him because he moved too fast for her, so she turned on him, white-faced.

'Why don't you leave me alone?' she broke out hoarsely.

'I will in a moment,' he returned in a chilly voice. 'But I wanted to remind you about this California trip. I think it's essential for you to come with us, and if you refuse I shall have to bring it up in the next board meeting. As a working director, I expect you to be part of whatever projects we tackle. Anyone else in your place would readily agree to join us on the trip. It's a reasonable request, after all. If you still refuse, give up your place on the board.'

Her green eyes flashed, but anger didn't help. Nick was leaving her no choice—she knew the rest of the board would see it his way, not hers. They wouldn't understand why she refused, and she couldn't explain, even though she knew Nick perfectly understood her reasons for not wanting to go to America with him.

'Very well, I'll come!' she said with stiff resentment.

He smiled, his eyes glittering with triumph. 'Now go and have that hot bath!' he commanded, turning on his heel and going towards his own front door.

Gina could have screamed. The expression of satisfaction on his face remained with her while she took her bath, dressed, and went down in the lift to the car park to drive into central London.

Nick liked getting his own way, especially with her. She knew how angry it made him when she denied him what he wanted. Nick could not bear rejection, refusal, being thwarted, but that was the very heart of her strategy of revenge, and it irritated her that he should have managed to get her into a position where she had had to give in to him over this American trip. It was a small enough victory, but she had seen from his face that Nick loved winning it. He would be insufferable over it for the next few days!

It was hard to find a parking place in central London on a Saturday night, but Gina knew she might find one around Covent Garden, which was within easy walking distance of the theatre she was going to that evening, and sure enough on her second circuit of the area she managed to park in a side-street off the market area. It was by then a quarter to seven, but there were still plenty of people about in Covent Garden and wandering along the Strand.

Gina had a light pre-theatre supper in a little restaurant nearby, an exotic fruit cocktail followed by chicken in a white sauce with mushrooms and grapes, served with salad. She just had time to have coffee after that, and then she hurried off to the theatre.

The musical was fast-moving, funny, full of good tunes, and Mac Cameron was marvellous. He could sing, dance, make you laugh, as well as act, and Gina was entranced throughout the first act. The rest of the audience obviously loved it, too. As they all moved out into the bars during the interval there was an excited buzz of comment. While she waited to get her fruit juice she listened to what people were saying.

'His voice is terrific! I must buy the album of the show.'

'He looks shorter than I'd expected!' said one teenager to her friend.

'You're crazy, Karen! He's at least six foot, and every foot of him looking good, too! I'd like to find him in my Christmas stocking, I can tell you!'

'Flora!' giggled the other girl. 'Someone will hear you.'

'I don't care!' said Flora, paying for their glasses of Coke. They went off with them and Gina got nearer to the counter.

'He's so good! Where does he get his energy? I never thought he could dance like that—did you, Jimmy?' a dyed blonde in front of her enthused.

'Especially at his age,' agreed the man beside her. He was bald, pink-faced, well-dressed, middle-aged.

'He's not that old! Early thirties, I'd say.'

'Early forties, more like! He's older than me!'

The blonde giggled. 'Who are you kidding, Jimmy!'

The bald man gave her a furious look, and turned away to order their drinks as the barman turned to him, and the blonde caught Gina's amused look, and winked at her.

Then it was Gina's turn and she asked for an orange juice mixed with mineral water in a tall glass; it was a long, refreshing drink and low-calorie, too. In the crowded theatre, it was very warm, and her throat was dry. She moved away from the counter and took a long swallow.

She had almost finished her drink when someone came up behind her and said her name.

'Gina? It is Gina Tyrrell, isn't it?'

She swung, startled, her green eyes wide. For a second she couldn't place the man smiling at her.

'It is Gina, isn't it?' he repeated and she nodded, smiling back as she suddenly remembered him.

'Yes, that's right. I haven't seen you for ages, Sir Dermot. Not since...' She broke off, realising that the last time they met had been Sir George Tyrrell's funeral. Indeed, she knew Sir Dermot Gaskell only because his father, Brendan Gaskell, had been at school with Sir George, who had become godfather to Brendan's first child and only son, Dermot. Brendan Gaskell had died years before Sir George. He had had a stroke when he was in his sixties, Gina had not even known him, but Sir George had always kept in touch with his godson, Dermot.

'Not since the old man died,' nodded Dermot, who was a very tall, very thin man in his early fifties, with thick grey hair and bright blue eyes. In spite of the grey hair, he gave the impression of youth because he was always lively and energetic. 'I miss him!' he added with a sigh, and Gina nodded.

'So do I.'

Sir Dermot had been on the board of the *Sentinel* before Nick Caspian took it over, but he had resigned in protest immediately after the death of Sir George, and Gina respected his stand, although she, herself, had decided to stay on the board and fight Nick from within. She had explained her decision to Sir Dermot at the time, and he had nodded approval. 'Well, I see your reasoning, but I have my doubts that you'll ever get anywhere. You're young, you don't know what you're up against. This Caspian fellow has got the paper now and I, for one, am not hanging around to watch while he destroys it. But I think the old man would have liked you to stand and fight. That would have been his way.' He had grimaced wryly. 'It isn't mine—maybe I'm wrong, but I'm going before I get pushed out, as I would be, sooner or later. Caspian doesn't want me. I'm a hangover from the Tyrrell era.'

'How are things on the *Sentinel* these days?' he asked Gina now, eyes shrewd. 'Won any fights yet?'

'Nick Caspian gets his own way most of the time,' she admitted and, when he grimaced, added, 'But now and then I have the odd victory, so I keep chipping away at him!'

'Good for you! Sir George would be proud of you!' He looked around the crowded bar. 'House full again tonight. We're coining money, while Mac is in the show.'

'We?' she repeated, puzzled.

Sir Dermot grinned, looking pleased with himself. 'I'm one of the angels.'

Gina stared blankly.

'I invested in this show,' he explained. 'I'm one of the backers—the theatre people call us angels. Just their little joke.'

'How interesting. Do you make a lot of money from investing in shows?' It had never occurred to Gina that someone had to put up the money to back a show, but now she thought that Sir Dermot was just the type to enjoy doing so. He had always been keen on the theatre and films.

'Not often,' he wryly said. 'One in three pays off, but I try to pick the shows that will run and run, naturally. That's where the skill comes in—if you have a good nose for what the public will go for, it gives you a better chance. You need luck, too, though. Once I knew Mac Cameron had signed to do this one, I jumped at the chance to invest in it, of course.'

'Have you met him? What's he really like?'

'He's a very friendly fellow.' Sir Dermot surveyed her, his eyes twinkling. 'Fan of his, are you? My wife and I are having a drink with him later, after the show. Why don't you join us? Very informal, just a drink in the green room. Bound to be a lot of people there, always is, but you might get a chance to talk to Mac.'

Gina hesitated, tempted yet uncertain. Sir Dermot obviously hadn't heard about the possible lawsuit, but when he introduced her to Mac Cameron what would the actor make of her being there so soon after his lawyer threatened the *Sentinel* management?

Sir Dermot would certainly mention her connection with the newspaper—wouldn't Mac Cameron suspect Nick Caspian had sent her? He might think she was there to soothe him down, make a private approach to him. He might jump to any number of conclusions—but she could be pretty certain that he would not think she was there by sheer coincidence.

'Thank you, Sir Dermot,' she said slowly, and he smiled paternally at her.

'My pleasure. We're in one of the boxes. Saw you in the front stalls, so tell you what—you wait in your seat and I'll come and fetch you and take you backstage with us.' He patted her shoulder. 'See you later, then.'

He vanished before Gina could get a word out, and while she was debating what to do the interval bell went and people began streaming back to their seats.

The curtain went up, the musical exploded into life again, and she gave herself up to delighted enjoyment of the show. There was no doubt about one thing—Mac Cameron was a star of amazing brilliance. When he was on stage you couldn't take your eyes off him and his sex appeal was breathtaking. Gina had seen him in films, but never on stage before. Now, she could understand why Molly Green had fallen for him at first sight.

When Sir Dermot came to fetch her, after the rest of the audience had headed for the exits, she was waiting. It might be crazy but she simply had to meet Mac Cameron and find out if he was as irresistible at close quarters as he was on a stage.

The party was in full swing when they got to it. They were handed a glass of champagne, courtesy of the management, and Sir Dermot and his wife, Shelley, took Gina around the crowded room introducing her to members of the cast and backstage technicians, not to mention a host of relatives and friends, and other theatrical 'angels'.

Gina kept glancing towards the charmed circle, mostly women, whose centre was Mac Cameron, no longer in make-up, his hair damp, as if he had showered since coming off stage, and wearing a black and gold silk dressing-gown.

Sir Dermot noted her frequent glances and laughed. 'Oh, come and meet him, my dear! He'll want to go soon, anyway, to change and get off to supper. He never eats before a show, says it makes him throw up—and afterwards he's starving!'

He took her hand and pushed their way through the throng towards the charmed circle, then, over the heads of those surrounding the actor, said in an authoritative voice, 'Isn't it time you went to change, Mac?'

Mac Cameron turned his hooded eyes that way, smiling. 'Is that an order, Dermot? How can I refuse?' He shrugged at his audience. 'Sorry, everyone—I must love you and leave you.'

'Ohh...no, not yet...it's early yet...' the women protested, giving Sir Dermot and Gina dagger-sharp looks of hostility.

'Love to stay all night, but I'm being torn away from you!' The actor's supple body was on the move already, towards the door, and Sir Dermot followed with Gina still held by the hand.

Then they were in a dark, cold corridor; Mac Cameron opened a door and paused in the flood of yellow light from the room within, turned to Sir Dermot and grinned lazily at him.

'Thanks for rescuing me! I'd have been there all night.'

'I thought you looked tired. Don't linger over supper tonight, Mac; get an early night for once.'

The actor laughed. 'I'm an owl, Dermot, I like to stay up all night and sleep until lunch, it suits me.' His eyes flicked to Gina, his brows rose sharply and he looked back at Sir Dermot. 'I thought I saw you with Shelley?'

'I am, she's in the party, waiting for me,' Sir Dermot said, amused. 'So don't you jump to wicked conclusions! Gina is a sort of a family friend...she's dying to meet you, so I brought her along.'

Gina was deeply embarrassed, but Mac Cameron smiled, holding out his hand, staring down into her slanting green eyes. 'Gina...it's a very musical name, and it suits you. I hope you enjoyed the show.'

'Oh, yes...' she said huskily, as his long fingers enclosed hers. 'The show was wonderful...' A pause, then she couldn't stop herself saying, 'And so were you.'

He didn't let go of her hand. 'Thank you,' he said, seriously, as if what she thought really mattered to him, which was ridiculous, of course, as they had only just met, and, anyway, he must have been told a million times how brilliant and stunning he was on stage.

'I didn't realise you were such a good dancer. In your films you haven't done much dancing, have you?'

'I haven't done a musical film yet,' he agreed. 'But I'm hoping they might make a film of this one. The trouble is, it takes so long to get a film into production—by the time they do make this one I may be too old to play the lead!' He grinned to show it was a joke, but she caught the darkness in his eyes and wondered if he worried about time passing and the threat of age.

Gently, she said, 'But you're such a marvellous actor that losing one part won't matter. You'll always be one of the cinema's big stars.'

His eyes widened and smiled again and he lifted her hand to his lips and kissed it lightly.

'I like you, Gina, you say all the right things!' he said, laughing. 'Why haven't I met you before? Look, have you eaten? I'm going on to supper—why don't you come?' He glanced at Sir Dermot, who had watched them with indulgence. 'And you and Shelley, too, of course!'

'No, Shelley and I hate staying up late, Mac, but by all means take Gina. I'll get back to Shelley now, my dear, enjoy yourself! Goodnight.'

'Oh, but...' she began, but Sir Dermot was walking away, down the dark corridor.

'Come and wait for me in here, while I get dressed,' Mac Cameron said, whisking her inside his dressing-room and shutting the door.

Gina froze on the spot, green eyes wide with distrust, and he gave her an amused grin.

'No need to look as if I'm offering a striptease!' he teased her. 'You can sit here, in my comfy chair.' He gave her a gentle push towards a shabby, sqashy old armchair, and she sank down into it, wondering if she would ever get out again. It was that sort of chair. Mac's eyes mocked her. 'And I'll dress behind this screen—and no peeking!'

While he was dressing her talked to her. 'What did old Dermot mean about you being sort of family?'

'My husband's grandfather was his godfather,' she warily told him, tense as she waited for him to ask her surname and realise then who she really was!

But he didn't, he said, 'Sounds complicated!' And then, in a sharp voice, 'Husband? You're married?'

'He's dead.'

'Oh. I'm sorry. How long ago...?'

'Six years now.'

'Six years?' His head appeared over the top of the screen, he stared at her. 'You must have got married while you were still at school!'

'We were both very young,' she admitted and, to her own surprise, heard herself adding, 'Too young. James was still a teenager in his head, he was reckless and wild, or he would never have had the accident that killed him.'

There was a silence, then Mac Cameron came out from behind the screen wearing elegant evening clothes, and looking so sexy in them that Gina had to fight the temptation to stare open-mouthed at him. He sat down at his dressing-table and began to brush his hair with silver-backed brushes. She watched, noting that his hair was thinning slightly at the front, but it didn't detract from his amazing looks.

'Did it put you off marriage?' he asked, looking back at her in the mirror.

The question startled her. 'Probably,' she slowly confessed, and knew that that was true, although she preferred not to probe too deeply into her own motives.

'Same here,' Mac said casually.

She was even more surprised by that, her eyes widening further. 'I didn't realise you had been married!'

'Yes, I got married in my teens, and it was a disaster. She's dead, too, now, not long ago, actually. We were divorced after a couple of years, and she married again, had a couple of kids. I heard she died of cancer last year.'

'How sad,' Gina said, watching him and wondering how the death had affected him.

He put away his hairbrushes and stood up, his face wry. 'It must have been, for her husband and children, but I must be honest. I barely remember her. I only remember the fights we had, the endless squabbling.' He looked at her, his eyes direct and very blue. 'Gina, I always warn girls before I date them, I don't want them to be under any illusions, or be able to reproach me later. I hated being married, and I made up my mind never to marry again. That isn't just a line I'm shooting, I mean it. I'm not the marrying kind. I hate responsibilities, and I hate having to go home to the same woman every night. I like your sex too much to want to be tied down by just one woman.' He slid his arms into a pale cashmere overcoat and turned to face her, one brow lifted. 'I've been frank with you, now it's up to you. If you aren't happy to date me, knowing how I feel, tell me now and we'll say goodnight and part friends.'

Gina considered him, her eyes gleaming with interest. 'How many times have you made that speech?' she asked, and laughed openly.

'Hundreds of times,' he admitted, grinning back at her.

'And they never believe you?'

'Some do. They call me a few names and walk out with their noses in the air.'

'But mostly they say they understand, and then hope to change your mind?'

He looked down into her teasing eyes. 'I like you, Gina...what is your last name?'

'Does it matter? As we're just ships passing in the night?'

Mac Cameron laughed. 'You're right. Let's just have fun and to hell with it.'

They swept out to the waiting limousine, pausing only so that Mac could sign a sheaf of autographs, then they drove through the brightly lit streets to a famous restaurant where Mac's appearance caused a little stir of excitement, craned necks, curious stares. Gina got some stares, too, but she was not a public figure, although her face had appeared in newspaper columns from time to time. She hoped nobody there recognised her.

Mac was ravenous, he said, but Gina explained that she had eaten at seven and wasn't really hungry.

'I'll order for us both, then, and you can eat or not, as you choose,' he said coolly, and told the water, 'My usual, Louis!'

'The soufflé tonight is kipper, Mr Cameron,' the waiter told him.

'My favourite! That's great.' Mac looked at Gina. 'Do you like kipper soufflé?'

'I don't think I've ever eaten it, but I love kippers.'

She did not think she would eat anything, but when a silver tureen of delicious consommé arrived she accepted a small bowl of that and finished it with pleasure, and simply couldn't resist the savoury soufflé.

While they ate and drank the excellent wines which were served with the meal, Mac talked and Gina listened. He was witty, fascinating, with an almost encyclopedic knowledge of the theatre and the cinema, but it was his hilarious anecdotes from his own career that she enjoyed most.

Once he paused to ask her politely, 'What did you say you do, Gina?'

'Oh, I just work in an office,' she hurriedly told him. 'Tell me more about that production of *Who Stabbed The Butler?*

She was having the time of her life, but she couldn't help wondering what Mac was like when you saw him every day. Was he always centre stage, performing? He wouldn't ever be boring, but Gina wondered if it might not get rather exhausting being an audience all the time.

He paid the bill at about one in the morning and they made their way to the door. The head waiter opened it for them and Mac put an arm round Gina to guide her out into the street. As he did so, a flashbulb exploded, then another. Dazzled and horrified, Gina stared at the shadowy cameraman before he vanished to the sound of running feet.

Mac wasn't drunk, but he was very cheerful after that excellent wine. 'The price of fame, I'm afraid, my dear! You are always on show. I've learnt to accept it with a sigh...' He looked rather pleased with himself, in fact, his ego boosted by the snatched picture, but he acted a heavy sigh. 'I just hope *you* don't mind appearing in the tabloids tomorrow?' he added mournfully.

Gina did. She minded very much indeed.

CHAPTER FOUR

VALERIE was still asleep in bed when her doorbell chimed. Yawning, she sat up, looked at her alarm clock, then did a double-take. It was six in the morning. The doorbell chimed again and she slid out of bed, grabbing up her silk wrap. Who on earth could be calling at this hour?

Nervously, she made sure the chain was latched before she opened the door and peered through a crack.

'You!' she breathed. 'What do you think you're doing, waking me up at this time of the morning?'

'Open up, Valerie,' Gilbey Collingwood said with grim terseness.

'I will not! You must be drunk. Go away.'

She tried to close the door again and he put his foot into the crack, then held up a newspaper, one of the *Sentinel*'s leading rivals, whose circulation was still way ahead of theirs. It was folded open at an inner page, prominently displaying a large, grainy photograph.

Valerie looked at the man in the picture first, recognised Mac Cameron at once and grimaced instinctively. 'Now what is he up to?' she said before she looked at the woman with him. Then her jaw dropped. 'That... that's...'

'Yes,' Gib said drily. 'It's Gina Tyrrell.'

Valerie stared at Gina's grey features in the newsprint. 'What on earth is she doing with him? I saw her yesterday morning, in Oxford Street—we talked about the case, and she was really nice to me. She didn't even breathe a word about knowing him!'

'Well, she does—no two ways about it! That is not a casual meeting. They'd just been dining alone together for hours, it seems, and look at the way he has his arm round her waist.'

Valerie looked. 'Why didn't Gina tell me?' she breathed, then a thought occurred to her. 'How did you get this, so early? Your paper boy must deliver at the crack of dawn.' She looked at him, her blue eyes narrowed. 'Come to that, what on earth are you doing up so early?'

'I've been to an all-night party...'

'I might have guessed,' she said with a bite in her voice, and he gave her a dry look.

'So you might. Always enjoying myself, I confess. Well, it was Saturday night, and I am young, free and single!'

'Did it make any difference to your lifestyle when you weren't?' she asked. 'Single, I mean?'

'If you'd stop shooting at me...' he complained and she shrugged.

'All right. So you went to another all-night party?'

He gave her a grim smile. 'Well, anyway, some time during the party I went to sleep in a chair, woke up with a stiff neck at around five o'clock, and decided to go home. On the way I stopped off at Barbary Wharf and collected a pile of papers to read with my breakfast, and this was the first one I glanced through, so I jumped back into my car and drove here. Now, will you open this door before one of your neighbours decides I'm trying to break in, and calls the police?'

She unlatched the door and fell back, and Gib walked past her into the sitting-room, which was filling with greyish light. Gib went over and drew the curtains back, but the sky was grey, too, and the room remained shadowy.

'I don't understand it—what was she doing dating him?' Valerie muttered.

Gib gave her a cynical look. 'What does any woman see in him? Apart, that is, from his good looks, fame and incredible wealth?'

'Gina Tyrrell doesn't need money, she isn't likely to be impressed by fame and I've never noticed her going overboard for any of the good-looking men around the office!' It was cold in here, and Valerie began shivering.

Gib bent down and switched on the electric fire. 'Why don't we have some coffee? That will wake you up, and help you think straight. I'll make it while you sit here and get warm again.' He glanced down over her thin silk wrap. 'That may look good, but it doesn't keep you warm, does it? You should get yourself a wool one.'

He was an odd man, he kept surprising her with unexpected facets of his character—beneath his cynicism and constant joking he hid kindness, warmth, gentleness.

She frowned. She didn't want to like him; he could be habit-forming. It could be tempting to lean on that strength of his, be comforted by his kindness, thought Valerie, a sigh wrenched out of her. Except that you couldn't lean on him, could you? He had walked out on one marriage—how would you ever be sure he wasn't going to walk out on you? You had to be absolutely certain about the man you chose, you only had one life and there was no point in wasting it on someone who might betray you, let you down, make a fool of you.

Her mother had warned her all her life to make sure she picked the right man, but in her teens she hadn't taken those warnings seriously, she had fallen in love with the first good-looking man she met. It had ended in disaster, just as her mother had prophesied, and Valerie had never laughed at her mother's warnings again.

'Can I see that paper?' she called after Gib, and he came back.

'Sure, that's why I brought it,' he told her, tossing it over, and switching on the light before he went out.

Valerie spread the newspaper out on her lap and stared at the picture, read the brief paragraph underneath.

Mac Cameron, currently starring in the West End's biggest musical hit, seen dining at top Mayfair restaurant last night with wealthy redheaded beauty, Gina Tyrrell, widow of the Tyrrell heir whose family once owned the *Sentinel* newspaper. Their mystery romance unfolds amid rumours that Mac threatens a million-plus lawsuit against *Sentinel* proprietor Nick Caspian, whose long-running feud with Gina is the gossip of Fleet Street. Friends denied all knowledge of her relationship with Mac. 'But she is very angry with Nick at the moment,' admitted one, however. 'Maybe this is her way of getting back at him?'

Gib came back with a tray of coffee and some slices of buttered toast. Valerie accepted a cup and a slice of toast, the newspaper slipping off her lap to the floor.

'They seem to be implying that...' She looked up at Gib, not quite able to put it into words.

He nodded. 'That Gina is somehow involved in Mac Cameron's lawsuit, that she's encouraging him to sue the paper, because of her feud with Nick. I know.'

Valerie bit absently into her toast. It was delicious. 'I can't believe she'd do that.'

Gib gave one of his cynical grins. 'Especially since she has a lot of shares in the paper, and wouldn't want to see it bled white by Mac Cameron and his gang of piratical lawyers! No. And however much she dislikes Nick Caspian, I wouldn't think there was any doubt about her loyalty to the *Sentinel*.'

'No...' Valerie slowly said, frowning, then looked at what was left of her slice of toast. 'This is buttered!' she said in tones of utter horror.

'Don't you like it?' he asked innocently.

She gave him a suspicious look. Had he done it deliberately? 'It's gorgeous, but butter is simply loaded with calories!'

'You need them, getting up at this hour!' urged Gib.

The thought struck her as brilliant. 'Yes, I do, don't I?' she said happily, finishing the toast before drinking her coffee, then she bent down to pick up the newspaper and stare at that photograph again.

'They do look ... well ...'

'Intimate?' asked Gib, coming over and taking a casual perch on the edge of her chair to peer at the picture, too.

'As if they like each other a lot,' Valerie corrected.

He was leaning over her shoulder, his cheek almost touching her hair, she felt him breathing, smelt the fresh air of an autumn morning on his skin. Slowly she stiffened in the chair, deeply conscious of him.

'You'll have to ask her,' Gib said.

She had lost the thread of the conversation. 'Ask her?' she repeated, looking up at him.

'How well she knows him!' Gib stared down into her eyes, their blue almost purple at that moment, darkened by feeling and confusion.

'Oh ... yes ...' she stammered, hypnotised, unable to look away.

'And why she didn't tell you she knew him,' Gib murmured, slowly bending towards her.

'Yes,' she said, staring at his mouth. She had never really looked at it before, never noticed the strength and warmth of it.

It softly touched her lips and part of her mind warned her to stop him now before this got out of hand, but some other part of her felt so weak, with the threat of this lawsuit, of losing her job, that she wanted to be kissed, needed some human warmth, the closeness of being held in someone's arms.

'Oh ... Valerie!' Gib suddenly groaned against her mouth, hoarseness in his voice. His arms went round her in a possessive grip, and she yielded to them in a trancelike state, not knowing for sure why she wasn't fighting him off as usual.

For the first time since they met, she wasn't pushing him away or scolding him, or trying to evade his searching mouth, and both of them were aware of it.

Gib was running one hand up and down her back, moulding her closer to him as he pressed her back into the cushioned upholstery, kissing her more and more passionately, his body arched over her. She felt heat coming from his skin, heard his thickening breathing, and suddenly grew frightened. Gib was sexually aroused, his excitement signalled by his mouth, his roving hands, the way his body moved against her.

She pulled her head back, flushed and trembling, and tried to sound angry, distasteful, as she had so often in the past. 'Stop it! How many times do I have to tell you I hate it when you touch me?'

Gib stiffened, staring at her fixedly, his skin darkly flushed, his breathing still audible. After a minute, he muttered, 'Why did you let me start kissing you, if you hate it when I touch you?'

'I ...' She was flustered and stammering. She couldn't admit the truth, that she had needed his kiss, the comfort of his arms. He wouldn't understand, and would only reach for her again. 'I ... was grateful ... you'd been kind ...'

'Grateful!' He threw the word back at her as if it were a hand grenade. 'My God, sometimes I can't believe you're real! What were you doing, then, rewarding me with a few kisses, so long as I didn't get too worked up over them and try to go too far?'

That was too close to the truth, and Valerie went white, her body helplessly shaking, unable even to deny it.

Gib stared, his eyes narrowing. 'God in heaven, you were!' he said in a flat, still voice, but she was not fooled by the apparent calmness in it. Gib was angry, violently angry. She saw it in the feverish brightness of those slitted eyes, in the cruel, sardonic line of his mouth.

She tried to get up, out of the chair, to get away, to escape to her bedroom, but as she moved Gib barred her way, his arm pushing her down into the chair.

'No, Valerie, this time you aren't running away!'

His voice scared her rigid, but she fought her fear down, put up her chin, tried to face him defiantly.

'Don't you threaten me! Get out of my flat, now, and leave me alone, or...'

'Or what?' he mocked, sliding down into the chair with her.

'You're hurting me!' she cried out as his lean, muscled body came down and crushed her backwards, but a second later his arm scooped her up as if she was as light as a feather and she found herself lying on top of him, her legs flung over the arm of the chair and her body held on his lap.

'Is that more comfortable?' he drawled.

She struggled, angrily, but all she achieved by that was to make her silk wrap fall open, leaving her legs bare to the thigh. He laughed, staring at the smooth, pale skin exposed, then his laughter stopped and he breathed in that thick, audible fashion, staring. His hand slid slowly downwards, over her silk-sheathed hips, and began to caress her naked thighs.

Until that instant she had been alert, warily on guard, but she hadn't really been frightened of what Gib intended. Now shock flashed through her. The way he was touching her now was disturbingly intimate. Gib was out of control.

His other hand was busy, too; untying the belt of her wrap and inserting itself, as sinuously as a snake, inside, searching for her breasts, cupping one in his palm, the hardening nipple pressing against his warmth. Her heart beat heavily within her ribcage. Through the thin silk of her nightdress she felt the heat of his hand, and desire spiked through her, made perspiration spring out on her temples.

Valerie did not know what to do, how to stop him, when she couldn't even fight the way she felt.

She hadn't changed her mind: she didn't want to risk caring about someone like Gib; she didn't want to take him seriously and she didn't want an affair with him. She just couldn't trust him. She certainly didn't want to end up in bed with him just because the way he touched her could make her feel a pleasure so sharp that it hurt.

But how could she make him stop when, whatever she might say, her body was giving him very different signals? How was she to call a halt?

The trouble was, in a straight fight, she would lose. He was bigger, stronger, and dangerously aroused. She had to do something, but what? She bit her lip, nervously staring up at his taut, flushed face, the glitter of his eyes.

Her mind was a blank; she couldn't think clearly, her body was too obsessed with sensations she had never felt before, wild stabs of pleasure, an intense, shuddering desire.

Another reporter, who had competed with her for a story which Valerie had got simply because she was by accident in the right place at the right time, had said bitterly that she must have been born under a lucky star, and her luck certainly held that morning.

Out of the blue, Gib abruptly raised his head and gave a loud sniff. 'What the . . . ?' he muttered, sitting up, and the next second Valerie found herself sprawling on the carpet while he leapt across the room like a crazy man.

Completely bewildered, she stumbled to her feet, tying her wrap tightly with hands that shook.

Only then did she realise what had made Gib act so oddly. The newspaper he had brought there that morning had fallen on the floor right next to the electric fire and must have been smouldering away for minutes on end before it finally burst into flames. The smell of burning paper had got through to Gib almost at once, luckily, and now he was busy stamping out the fire.

Valerie groaned as she saw the blackened mess on her pale pink carpet.

'Oh, no! My carpet! It's ruined!' She turned on Gib, glaring. 'It's all your fault. You're a walking disaster area—whenever you come near me something dreadful happens. I should never have let you through the door!'

'I'm sorry, Valerie,' he said, trying to placate her.

'Oh, yes, it's easy to say sorry. I've only just bought that carpet!'

'I'll pay for it to be cleaned! Oh, come on, Valerie, I didn't do it deliberately. It was an accident—you can't blame me for it.'

'Can't I?' she asked coldly. 'Well, of course, if you say so, you must be right. Now, I think you had better go. I'll have to clear up that mess before I go to work.'

'I'll do it.' His face was set and angry, too, by now. When he looked like that he was alarming, quite different, but she refused to be intimidated by the way he was looking at her.

'No, just get out of here, will you?'

'You're using this as an excuse,' he said, staring hard at her. 'Aren't you? You couldn't be this angry about your damn carpet!'

She walked away without answering, and opened the front door of her flat. For one second she thought he was going to refuse to leave, argue with her, then he walked past her in frowning silence, and she closed the door on him before he could change his mind and try to come back.

What she wanted to do then was lie down on her bed, because she felt depressed and tired, and close to tears, although she wasn't sure exactly why—but she had too much to do, and Valerie was far too sensible to give in to her own stupid feelings.

Instead, she got to work on the carpet, removed the unburnt part of the newspaper before delicately picking up by hand most of the blackened, ashy remainder, except for the fragments Gib had stamped into the deep pink pile. It took her some time to brush all of them out into a dustpan before she vacuumed the whole room.

In front of the electric fire there was still a noticeable burn mark, however. She sighed and hunted out a bottle of carpet cleaner. That made a difference, but with a sigh of irritation she realised that she was never going to shift that stain.

Valerie was quite houseproud. It really irked her to know that the ash-grey mark would always mar the pastel pink of her new carpet. Putting her cleaning things away, she went to have a shower and got dressed, still in a grim mood.

Although it was Sunday and most people did not work, that didn't apply to journalists on daily newspapers. They had to work on Sundays to put together a paper for Monday morning. The features page, however, largely relied on stories which had been written in advance, so that features writers did not need to work at weekends, but Valerie decided to visit the Green family home and persuade them to tell her where to find Molly.

They lived in Finchley in a very ordinary street of houses built between the two world wars. By the time Valerie got there, it was half-past ten, and Mr Green was in the front garden pruning his rose trees. It was a well-kept garden: a small, well-mown lawn, a few shrubs, a cluster of chrysanthemums, russet and white and orange-gold, and the rose trees which were still flowering, dark red and fragrant blooms.

Mr Green was a small, thin, neat man with a little grey moustache. He looked round at the click of the front gate and his face tightened with hostility.

'You're that reporter, the one who started all this——'

'I didn't twist Molly's arm, she wanted to tell me her story!' Valerie quickly protested.

'And ever since you printed it our lives have been a misery!'

'I'm very sorry about that...'

'Are you? Are you really?' he sneered, picked up a trug full of dead-headed roses and started towards his front door.

'Please, Mr Green, listen, it is really urgent that I talk to Molly today. Mac Cameron says——'

'Don't mention his name to me!' Mr Green burst out, flushing dark and angry red. 'Go away, will you? Haven't you done enough? Yesterday we had reporters climbing all over this garden, knocking at the door, ringing the bell, peering through the windows, talking to our neigh-

bours. Anyone who hadn't read your dreadful newspaper heard heaven alone know what lies from them!'

Valerie couldn't blame him for being so furious; from
his description of the scene her Fleet Street colleagues
had been more than usually insensitive and downright
brutal.

'I know how you must feel——' she began, and he
interrupted, his moustache bristling in a way which would
have been comic if he had not been so upset.

'I wish you did! I wish it would happen to you one
day! It was the worst experience of my life, and my wife
was distraught. I called the police and they came along,
but they said there was nothing they could do except ask
them to leave, and they did, but as soon as the police
had gone the reporters all came back. My wife's ill with
the worry of it.' He opened his front door and snarled
at Valerie, 'Now, clear off, will you, and don't come
back!'

Before he could get inside and shut the door on her,
she desperately got out, 'Mac Cameron is suing the paper
for a fortune!'

Mr Green paused, looking back at her. 'He's what?'

'He says Molly is lying, the baby isn't his.'

The man's face whitened, then turned brick-red. He
swore violently and Valerie could not blame him.

'Now do you see why I have to talk to Molly?' she
quietly asked.

From the house a voice whispered, 'Give him her address, Tom.'

He looked into the shadowy hallway. 'I don't want
her pestered!'

'That man isn't getting away with calling my daughter
a liar!' Mrs Green said with choked intensity, and Valerie
saw her, then, standing in the hall, in a blue velvet
dressing-gown, her hair tousled, as if she had been in

bed when she heard her husband arguing with Valerie
and had come down to hear more clearly.

'I swear I won't tell anyone else the address,' Valerie
said quickly, seeing Mr Green waver. 'I understand why
you're so angry, I realise that what we printed stirred
up a hornets' nest for you and Molly, and I really do
regret that. You've had a very bad time, but remember
she chose to talk to me, she wanted me to print her story
in my paper. She trusted me, and I wrote the article
honestly, I didn't make up anything, I used her own
words, and I've got everything we both said, on tape,
so I can prove I didn't misquote her.'

The two of them stared at her. Mrs Green sighed. 'Give
her the address, Tom.'

'We should ring Molly first and ask if it's OK!' her
husband protested.

'Go and ring her now, then.'

'If I could talk to her on the phone, I could make her
see why I need to talk to her!' Valerie quickly said.

'Maybe it would be enough for you talk to her on the
phone and you wouldn't need to see her?' Mr Green
suggested rather hopelessly.

Valerie knew it wouldn't. She had to see Molly, look
into that clear, wide-eyed face again, try to assess the
real character of the girl.

'If I can talk to her, we might be able to sort something out!' Her answer was evasive, and she saw from
his expression that he knew it, but she didn't want an
argument with him, or his wife. They were both wary,
both hostile, both uncertain and worn out with the
badgering they had got from the Press since her article
appeared.

Mr Green walked into the house and she followed him.
The front door was shut and she listened to the telephone ringing. Mr Green put his trug of dead roses down

on the floor and picked up the telephone. He listened
for a second; hung up again.

'That's something else you started!' he told her bitterly. 'Dirty phone calls. The minds some people have
got! We ought to have the phone cut off, but we need
it now more than ever—we don't dare go out in case
they come back, so we must have the phone to keep in
touch.'

He began to dial before the ringing could start up
again. 'Hello, Janet,' he said after a moment. 'Tom here.
How are you? Good. And Andy?' He listened, sighing.
'Well, you know, we're having a difficult time, but we're
bearing up. Oh, we'll cope, don't worry.' He sounded
stronger than he looked. 'Is Molly around? Yes, I'd like
to talk to her, thanks.'

Valerie waited, watching him. For the first time in her
career she was feeling guilty, although she kept telling
herself she had only been doing her job. She hadn't intended to hurt these people, or their daughter. In fact,
if anyone was to blame, it was Mac Cameron, not her!

'Molly, love, it's Dad,' said Mr Green affectionately,
then stopped, listening. 'Now, don't you worry about
us, we're fine,' he said after a moment. 'Just you look
after yourself. That's all we care about. How are you?
Feeling any better?' He listened, half smiling. 'You
always did love it on the farm, didn't you? When you
were tiny and stayed with Aunt Helen. Do you good,
down there, I said, didn't I? And I was right. And you're
best out of it. None of them have found you, then? Well,
thank heavens for that.' He paused, took a deep breath.
'Molly, love, just one problem . . . he's threatening to sue
the *Sentinel*, he says it isn't his baby . . . Well, you know
what he says. Now he's making it legal, dear. And that
lady reporter wants to talk to you, and I think you'd
better. She's here now, shall I put her on?'

Valerie moved closer, as he listened again. He turned and held the phone out to her.

'Hello, Molly,' she said. 'How are you?'

The girl's voice was husky, troubled. 'What do you think?'

'I'm glad you're having a peaceful holiday. And I'm really sorry to bother you, Molly, I wouldn't if I could help it, but... Well, your father told you the problem, so I won't waste time explaining that, but I need to see you at once. My paper is going to fight him, we're backing you to the hilt, we believe you're telling the truth and he's the liar. But I must see you to go over the story again to make sure every detail is accurate so that our lawyers have the ammunition they need if they're going to beat him. You do want him to lose this case, don't you, Molly? If he gets away with it you'll never be able to get him to admit paternity, and you won't get a penny from him, for your baby.'

'I don't care about that!' Molly said furiously. 'I don't want his money, but he isn't getting away with saying I sleep around, that he wasn't the only man in my life, because it's lies. There was nobody else, and he is the father of my baby!'

'I believe you! But I must see you and we must go over the whole story to see if we can work out a defence!'

Molly didn't say anything for a second or two, then she sighed heavily. 'I don't seem to have much choice, do I?'

'I promise I'll try not to be too much of a nuisance, and I won't tell anyone where you are.'

Molly gave her the address of the farm where she was staying, and told her how to get there from the nearest motorway.

'I'll come down this afternoon, I can't say for sure what time I'll get there, but you will be there all day?' Valerie asked, and Molly laughed with a rough cynicism.

'Where else can I go? I'm afraid of being recognised if I leave the farm. I even hide when my cousins get any visitors.'

'Well, don't hide when I arrive, will you?' Valerie said lightly. 'See you later. I'll put your father on again...' She turned and handed the telephone back to Mr Green, who began talking to his daughter. Quietly, Valerie said goodbye to his wife, and opened the front door to leave.

As she did so, someone darted forward and she found herself blinking into a camera lens, blinded by a flash, and then another. For a second she couldn't see, then she saw the men on the path, surging forward, trying to get into the house. Mrs Green must have seen them because the front door suddenly slammed shut, leaving Valerie engulfed in reporters and cameramen.

Several of them knew her. 'It's Val Knight, Caspian the Barbarian's favourite reporter,' one explained to the others who all laughed at the description of Nick Caspian. Valerie couldn't help laughing, too; she hadn't heard that one before, and it was good; she must repeat it when she got back to Barbary Wharf. They'd love it.

'What gives, Val?' asked Benny Howell, the humorist who had coined the phrase, a young man in his twenties, with a muscular build and a head of rough, curly brown hair. 'Why are you here? Something happen?'

'Got a new lead?' another man shouted.

'Have the *Sentinel* got the girl salted away?' asked someone else, and then there was a babble of questions from all the others.

Valerie started trying to push her way through them, but they jostled and pushed back, and she felt a flutter of panic, for the first time realising how it felt to be on the receiving end of this treatment.

Benny suddenly put an arm around her and used his muscle to force his friends back, rushed with her through them and out on to the pavement.

'Thanks,' she breathlessly said, surprised by his unexpected chivalry. 'That's my car.' She unlocked it and Benny held the door while she slid inside, but he didn't stand back to let her drive off, he ran round to the other side of the car while she was starting the engine, and before she could drive off he was getting into the passenger seat.

'Hurry up, let's go!' he urged as the others surged around her car.

There was no time to argue. She shot away, almost knocking down a couple of reporters, who just jumped out of the way in time. As she turned the corner out of the ordinary little street she saw cars following them.

'Lose them, sweetheart,' Benny told her out of the corner of his mouth.

She gave him a dry sideways glance. 'This is not a gangster film.'

He grinned. 'Pity, I was just fancying myself as Humphrey Bogart.'

'I noticed.' Valerie headed south again and her little tail of cars followed her. There wasn't much traffic around, it being Sunday morning, and her escort stayed in place without a problem.

'Where are we going?' Benny asked, looking out of the window with a frown.

'Wait and see,' she said, smiling.

He turned to look at her. 'I've been meaning to ask you for a date for years, but never got you alone. Now here we are ... just the two of us ... so, will you have dinner with me one night?'

Valerie kept her eyes on the road. 'Sorry, Benny, I'm in a serious relationship, no outside dates.'

'The Spanish guy?'

Her face tightened at the mention of Esteban. 'No.'

'Don't tell me you've finally let Gilbey Collingwood catch up with you?' Benny laughed and she flushed slightly. If Benny knew Gib had been chasing her for ages, then everyone in Fleet Street knew, and she resented that.

'My private life is my business!' she snapped, turning down towards the Thames.

Benny looked out of the window, frowned, then swore. 'You're making for Barbary Wharf, aren't you?' he guessed at last and she laughed.

'I'm afraid they won't let you in without a pass,' she teased. 'I'll have to let you off before I go down into the car park. You can get a bus round the corner, or a taxi. You didn't leave your car outside the Greens' house? It's going to take you ages to get back there on a bus; better take a taxi. I hope your paper doesn't ask too many questions when you hand in your expenses sheet.'

'You little...' Benny called her names, but she just smiled.

'Did I ask you to get into my car? Thanks for the rescue, anyway, you're a knight in shining armour, even if you did have an ulterior motive.'

She pulled up at the entrance to the Barbary Wharf car park, looking into her driving mirror. The other cars had already peeled away and driven off in disgust, having recognised the area at last.

'Out you get, Benny.'

'You do owe me something,' he said, turning towards her, his arms going behind her and his body a threat poised like a snake about to strike.

'Get out of my car!' she repeated, staring angrily back.

He came at her, holding her down as she tried to fight him off, and she wrenched her head aside so that he couldn't kiss her, punched him, struggled violently.

It didn't take much of that for Benny to give up, muttering under his breath. He ran a hand over his curly hair, threw her a hostile look and got out of the other door. Valerie didn't wait around, she drove straight down into the car park, halting only to show her security pass to the man on duty. The pole lifted and she drove through the car park to her personal parking bay. They were all numbered, and unless you were allotted a bay and had the card to prove it you wouldn't be allowed past the security man.

She sat in her car for a few minutes, feeling rather shaky. She was sick and tired of having to fight men off. It had been fun, once, to have such a sexy image it had made her feel good, but now she was no longer enjoying the attention she got. It made her feel like an object, fruit on a market stall, always being grabbed and fondled.

She hated it. This morning it had been Gib, just now it had been Benny. What made them think they could do that to her? Tears pricked her eyes. She wanted to be loved, not lusted after; she wanted to be cherished, not grabbed. She ran a shaky hand over her wet eyes and sniffed, then got out her make-up bag and inspected herself in her compact mirror. She looked a mess, pink eyes, runny mascara, hair all over the place where Benny had handled her. She tidied herself up, locked her car and went up in the lift to the editorial floor to talk to the features editor.

Before she went to see Molly, she had better tell Colette what she planned to do, in case of repercussions. Anyway, there was no point in leaving just yet. She might find herself being followed by one of the other reporters in the hope of being led to Molly.

Colette grimaced, after listening to Valerie's story of her visit to the Greens and the subsequent chase.

'You must have someone with you, to do the driving while you keep out of sight. You'll have to sit in the back with a blanket over you until you've got well away from here.'

'I'll feel stupid!'

'Never mind that. Better take a photographer—he can drive.'

Valerie shook her head. 'No, definitely not. Molly wouldn't like it, she might not even see me if I came down with a photographer.'

Colette gave her a wry look. 'Don't go soft on me, Val, just because you're sorry for the kid. We're in a circulation war, and there are always casualties in a war. Your job is to write what will sell papers; you aren't employed as an agony aunt.'

Valerie stubbornly said, 'The lawyers want me to see Molly and check with her again. If I take a photographer down there, she'll duck out on me. So save the battle speeches. Just let me do my job my own way.'

Colette shrugged. 'OK. Do it your way, but if the editor asks for pictures I am not taking the blame when I tell him there are none. Which reminds me, did you see——?'

'The picture of Gina Tyrrell with Mac Cameron?' interrupted Valerie. 'Yes, I couldn't believe my eyes. Why didn't she say she knew him? Do you think there's anything going on? I mean...'

'Everyone's talking about it today, but Gina isn't around, so it's all guesswork and rumour!'

'I wonder how Nick Caspian took it?'

'God knows. Apparently, he flew off to Stockholm yesterday and nobody knows when he'll be back, so he may not even know yet.'

'I'd like to be a fly on the wall when he sees it. Sometimes they're at each other's throats in the office in front of everyone!'

'I think he fancies her,' Colette said, grinning.

Valerie nodded. 'Oh, yes, that's obvious. Hey, guess what I heard someone call him today? Caspian the Barbarian.'

Colette laughed. 'I like it! I can just see him in a leopardskin loincloth swinging through the trees.'

'That's Tarzan. Conan the Barbarian goes around half-naked, though, and our Nick would probably strip quite nicely.'

They both grinned, then Colette said soberly, 'I think you'd better check with the lawyers before you see Molly, you know. They may have questions they want answered.'

'I'll ring them now, then.'

'Use my phone,' invited Colette, and Valerie picked it up and dialled.

Sophie Watson answered the phone in her cool, clear voice and Valerie flatly asked to speak to Guy Faulkner.

'He's in a meeting at the moment, and so is Mr Sandel. Can I give them a message?'

Valerie explained why she had rung, and Sophie said, 'I'll tell them the minute they are free. Perhaps you shouldn't leave until they get back to you? They should finish this meeting in half an hour.'

'Yes, OK,' Valerie said, 'I'll be on Extension 321.' She hung up and Colette gave her a curious glance.

'You don't like Sophie, do you?'

'Does it show?'

'Your face and voice turn cold whenever you talk to her,' Colette said, smiling. 'What has she done to you?'

'Nothing. I don't know why I don't like her,' Valerie lied, going back to her own desk to wait for the call from the legal department.

She certainly wasn't admitting that she did not like Sophie Watson because Gilbey Collingwood did. In any case, it was inexplicable. She couldn't be jealous, because she was not in love with Gib, so why should it matter to her what he did? Why did it make her stomach clench and her teeth grate, to imagine him with Sophie? Or with any other girl, come to that? She couldn't even bear to think of him with his ex-wife, who hadn't lived with him for years, he claimed.

She got out her notes on Molly Green and read through them for around the twentieth time since she heard of Mac Cameron's threat. The phone rang, and she picked it up absently.

It was Guy Faulkner, his voice smooth and warm. 'I gather you've tracked Molly Green down and plan to see her today? Good. There are one or two questions you could put to her.'

'Yes, Mr Faulkner?'

'Call me Guy, Valerie,' he said softly, then explained what he wanted her to ask Molly. Valerie made notes in her pad, grimacing at some of the questions.

'She may not answer—that last one was pretty personal.'

'With that much money at stake, we'll need to get pretty personal, I'm afraid. In court, it could be worse.'

Valerie sighed. 'I suppose you're right. OK, I'll do my best.'

'I'm sure you will, Valerie,' he said, a smile sounding in his voice. 'When you get back, maybe we could have lunch and discuss the case? There are a number of questions I want to go over with you.'

'Fine, it's a date,' she said. 'See you when I get back, then, Guy.'

She put the phone down, still smiling, and only then realised that she had had an audience during some part of the phone call.

Gib was leaning against the empty desk next to her, his arms folded, and a frown on his face.

Valerie stiffened. 'What are you doing there, eavesdropping on my phone calls? I'm working, this is confidential stuff I'm dealing with...'

'Like making a date with Guy Faulkner?' he bit out contemptuously. 'You keep telling me what high principles you've got. You won't date me because I'm divorced, but you date Faulkner, who's engaged to marry someone else! Your standards baffle me. Or is it because Guy Faulkner has a big private income as well as his salary?'

CHAPTER FIVE

VALERIE flushed, her mind swamped by a muddle of reactions—rage, insulted pride, surprise. For a minute she was so taken aback that she just stammered, confused and furious.

'I...you...that's...is that what you think? That I'm only after money? You just tell yourself that to soothe your ego! Well, you're wrong! If you were a millionaire I wouldn't go out with you.'

'Thank you,' he said through his teeth, his skin turning dark red.

She was glad if that had pricked his thick skin. 'And I don't believe you about Guy,' she snapped. 'I never heard of any engagement, and if he was engaged someone would have mentioned it!'

'I was right about Esteban,' he drawled, and she bit her lip.

'Except that his wife was dead!' she flung back, blue eyes fierce.

'Guy's fiancée isn't dead,' he told her triumphantly. 'I know her. Harriet Ridgeway, she's a barrister, although you'd never guess it, to look at her—she manages to look about nineteen, although she's actually around twenty-five. Big brown eyes, like pansies, lots of curls...'

'Very poetic,' Valerie said viciously. 'Sure it's Guy, not you, who's dating her?'

His eyes gleamed and she hoped he hadn't picked up the note of jealousy in her voice.

'Unfortunately, he saw her first. They met at law school, but decided not to get married until they were both well established. Harriet is keen on her career; she means to go on with it after she marries Guy.'

Valerie still wasn't convinced. 'So how do you know her?'

'She lives next door to me; we first chatted over the garden wall.'

'You garden?' Valerie's voice was loaded with disbelief and Gib grinned.

'Not exactly. I looked out of my garden window and saw this vision, sunbathing in a bikini, so...'

'You don't need to draw a diagram, I can imagine the rest!' Only too well. Valerie knew what a flirt he was.

Gib smiled narrowly at her. 'She told me she was engaged, that first day, to a lawyer on the *Sentinel*. Quite a coincidence. You should have seen her face when I told her I worked there too! Since then, I've given her a few tips on buying shares. Her family have money, her father is a judge—you must have heard of him, Judge Ridgeway is always hitting the headlines. He has very right-wing views and gives pretty heavy sentences. Harriet left home to get away from him, I think, they don't seem to get on, but she said he was pleased about her engagement to Guy because the Faulkner family are so wealthy.'

Valerie frowned. 'Guy told me he had worked his way through law school and knew how to live on next to nothing a week!'

'Maybe his family refused to support him?'

'I suppose so,' she slowly said, then saw Colette bearing down on them, her face impatient.

'Have you talked to the lawyers yet?' Colette demanded and Valerie nodded.

'They think I should go, and gave me a list of questions to ask Molly. I'm not too happy about some of them, they're very personal...about her and Mac

Cameron in bed, asking for details of what they did, and how he treated her...she'll be embarrassed by them, I'm sure of that.'

'Just ask her the questions, Val, and see what reaction you get,' said Colette. 'And you'd better get down there now, or you'll never make it back tonight. Have you found someone to drive you?'

'No, but I thought...I could sort of disguise myself...I've got a headscarf, to hide my hair, I could put on dark glasses too, maybe take off all my make-up...I'd rather do that than hide in the back of the car under a blanket!'

Colette looked doubtful. 'They may recognise your car.'

'I'll drive her,' Gib said coolly.

'No!' Valerie snapped.

Colette looked at him thoughtfully. 'What about your work? You can't just walk out.'

'I'm off duty today—I came in to see someone, but I'm off until Tuesday.'

'Then that's great, thanks!' smiled Colette.

'No, I don't want him driving me!' Valerie protested, appalled at the thought of driving so far, alone with Gib. She had successfully kept him out of her life for months, but lately he seemed to be there whenever she looked up, and it worried her, not least because she was thinking about him far too much.

Colette gave her an impatient stare. 'Why are you always arguing? You don't want to ask Molly personal questions, as if that wasn't what you were paid for, heaven knows! You don't want a photographer, you don't want someone to drive you there, you want this and you don't want that! Your job is to get to Molly Green and make sure this newspaper isn't going to lose a fortune over her. Stop making difficulties, and get on with your job—or you'll find yourself looking for another one! Gib will drive you, you will hide in the back under a blanket until you're sure you aren't being followed by the opposition, and you'll come back with everything the lawyers need for their case. Right?'

She held Valerie's eyes, frowning, and Valerie stiffly said, 'Right,' with angry reluctance.

Colette turned on her heel and walked off. Ignoring Gib, Valerie grabbed up her bag, stuffed into it her notepad and pens, her audio recorder and spare tapes, put on her sunglasses, tied a midnight-blue scarf over her hair, and began walking towards the lift very fast.

Gib kept pace with her casually, and didn't say a word, to her mingled relief and regret.

She would have liked him to say something she could react to—she wanted to hit him, for being there, for offering to drive her, for refusing to go away however many times she told him to get lost. At the same time, she was relieved that he didn't because she knew her temper was on such a hair trigger at that moment that she would have made a public scene: hit him or yelled at him, without caring who heard her or what gossip it would cause.

She was afraid, too, of how Gib would behave then. He might yell at her, if provoked enough he might slap her back, or, even worse, kiss her, making everyone think they were watching a lovers' quarrel. Gib would enjoy making the office think that!

He took advantage to every chance to get closer to her, and their relationship was becoming far too intimate for her peace of mind. He was turning up in her life with increasing frequency, finding out more and more about her, things she did not want him to know, like how to make her shake like a leaf by kissing the back of her neck, how to make her feel faint with pleasure by touching her in a certain way in a certain place.

Of course, she was finding out a lot about Gib, too; the way his skin creased around those teasing hazel eyes, when he smiled; his spurts of temper, his tolerance and sense of humour, the way he breathed when he was aroused. She knew Gib very well, now, but that was dangerous, as well, because the more she knew him the more she liked him and she did not want to feel so strongly about a man she didn't quite trust.

It was disturbing, and Valerie was scared. Perhaps Gib guessed that, because he didn't speak at all while they were in the lift going down to the underground car park, or even when they reached her car.

Then he said, 'Just to make doubly sure, we'll go in my car. Nobody will recognise that, and I've got a car rug.' He walked over to the dark red Jaguar, with Valerie slowly following him. Gib unlocked his car, picked up a soft, tartan wool rug from the back seat and said, 'Crouch down in the back, and I'll put this over you.'

'I'm not playing stupid games!' she said in a sulky voice. 'Benny and the others will have given up by now and gone.'

'And if they haven't?' Gib looked at her drily and she glared back, hesitating, then growled at him.

'Oh, all right.'

She climbed into the back of the car and crouched down in front of the soft leather seats; Gib flung the folds of his rug over her head.

'I shall suffocate!' she complained, pushing it off her face.

'No, you won't.' Gib rearranged the rug. 'Just keep down until we're well away from here and I'm sure we aren't being followed.'

She heard him climb into the front and the engine started, with a roar. Valerie was very uncomfortable; it was stifling under the folds of the woollen rug and this was not a position she wanted to hold for very long, or her back would soon start aching.

It seemed like an eternity until the car slowed and stopped, and Gib said in an amused voice, 'OK, you can come out now.'

She threw back the blanket, unfolded herself, feeling like a concertina, and looked out of the car window. He had parked in a lay-by on the road going west out of London; traffic surged past them.

'Nobody followed us, I double-checked, don't worry,' Gib said. 'Going to join me?'

She got out of the back of the car and into the front, beside him, and he started the engine again. He drove fast but she noticed that he only took calculated risks— he was a good driver, quick-thinking and expert at handling the car. For a while neither of them said anything, then they passed a sign for Winchester and he said, 'I've got an aunt in Winchester, we could stop for a cup of tea.'

'There isn't time,' Valerie said before she realised it was a joke, then she said, 'Do your family all come from the west country?'

'My parents live in Shaftesbury now, but they moved there after my father retired. He worked for the Bank of England, in Threadneedle Street, all his life, and we lived in Highgate when I was young, but my mother always longed to live in the country and we took holidays down in Dorset. She was a big Hardy fan and liked to visit all the places you can identify in the books. I just like to ride and swim, and my father played golf, so Dorset suited us all.'

'Have you got brothers and sisters?'

'One of each. My brother is a doctor in a busy hospital in Leeds and my sister works in an advertising agency, doing art work. Neither of them is married yet. Jimbo never has time and Alice is having far too much fun being single.'

'They're younger than you?'

He nodded. 'I came first, then four years later Jimbo arrived.'

'What's his real name? James?'

Gib grinned. 'Jamieson. I told you, my mother is romantic—she likes unusual names.'

'Alice isn't unusual. Rather old-fashioned, but not unusual.'

'Ah, but Alice wasn't the name Mother gave her. She calls herself Alice, but her real name is Hecuba.'

Valerie giggled. 'You're kidding.'

He shook his head. 'Afraid not. I was ten when she arrived and I remembered being horrified. Jimbo and I advised Alice to change her name before she started school, and since *Alice in Wonderland* was her favourite book...' He shrugged and Valerie giggled again.

'You seem to come from a very eccentric family.'

'Dad isn't eccentric, or romantic; he's very down to earth, you'll like him.'

She fell silent at this assumption that she would be meeting Mr Collingwood.

'What about your family?' Gib asked her. 'Where do they live?'

'Buckhurst Hill, in Essex,' she said shortly, not wishing to tell him too much about herself and her background.

'Isn't that near Epping Forest, around ten miles out of London?'

She nodded. 'Well, it's almost part of London now, but when I was small it still had a village atmosphere, and, thank heavens, they can't build on the forest, although they have cut roads through it.'

'You grew up there? What does your father do?'

She hesitated and he shot her a narrow-eyed glance. 'Is he still alive?'

'Yes,' she said curtly. 'But my parents were divorced when I was seven, and I've no idea where he is now.'

'Ah!'

The sharp little sound made her flush and scowl. 'What does that mean?'

'Come on, you know what it means!' Gib said flatly. 'I always wondered why you were so dead against divorce, now I know. It hit you hard when your father left, you've never got over it. Did your mother marry again?'

'Yes, and I'm very fond of my stepfather, before you start jumping to any more conclusions,' she said furiously. 'He's been more of a real father to me than my own, and I've always called him Dad.'

'So the second marriage has been happy?' Gib asked.

'Yes!' she snapped. 'They're very happy together, and have been for the past twelve years. I lived at home until I earned enough money to afford a flat of my own nearer the office, and I still visit them as often as I can.'

'No need to be so defensive!' he drawled. 'Do you get your looks from your mother?'

'Yes, I suppose so,' she said, still frowning, then broke out, 'And the way I feel about divorce isn't the simple question you seem to think it is! Yes, I hated it when my parents split up and my father walked out of my life. I was hurt because I'd adored him and I'd thought he loved me, but after the divorce I only saw him a few times, very briefly, then he stopped coming. He just forgot all about me, as if I were a toy he'd grown out of. But I gradually got over that, especially after my mother married again. My stepfather was such a nice man, very kind and good-hearted; he made us into a family again. And then I grew up and was stupid enough to fall for someone who turned out to be married, although he didn't tell me until too late. I got hurt, his wife got hurt, and, even worse, to me, his children got hurt, because there was a lot of scandal which they heard about. And that was when I made up my mind never to get involved with a married man again.'

Gib was silent for a while, then he said quietly, 'But I'm not married, any more, and my ex-wife has already married again and expects a baby any minute now.'

Valerie stared straight ahead, feeling miserable. 'I know...I know...but...it doesn't make any difference. I still think of you as a married man.'

'That's crazy!' He was getting angry with her now.

'All the same, I do,' she said flatly. 'Maybe it wasn't your fault the marriage broke up, but you were married, you belonged to another woman, I couldn't bear to live with the thought of that. I'd always feel you didn't belong to me, I'd stolen you.'

'For heaven's sake, Val!' he burst out, looking at her as if he wanted to strangle her, and the car veered sideways while his attention was elsewhere.

There was a loud blare from a car horn and they both jumped, their eyes flashing back to the road situation. Only then did they realise that another car had been in the act of passing them when the Jag started sidling sideways. There had very nearly been a crash. The other car had pulled back behind them again, but the driver was angrily hooting as they drove on.

Gib made an apologetic gesture to the other man, whose car zoomed past a moment later, still hooting.

'Don't talk, just drive, Gib,' Valerie said wearily.

'Sooner or later we are going to have to talk, though,' he told her with grim determination.

She shut her eyes and concentrated on what she had to ask Molly Green. Half an hour later, Gib said, 'I don't know about you, but I'm starving. I'm going to stop for a late lunch. It's a quarter to two, but they might still be serving lunch, and if not I'm sure they would make us some sandwiches.'

'I'd rather get to this farm as soon as possible, and skip lunch,' Valerie said, opening her eyes just in time to see him driving off the motorway on to a country road. 'Hey, where are you going?'

'I know an old pub just a couple of miles from here where they do wonderful meals.'

'I'm not hungry!'

'Well, I am.' Gib drove on, ignoring her protests, and ten minutes later pulled into the car park of a large Georgian coaching inn. Sulkily Valerie followed him into the restaurant, and, despite her claim not to be hungry couldn't resist the lure of the enormous menu. She ate melon and grilled fish with a salad, but Gib ordered smoked mackerel with horseradish sauce followed by steak, kidney and oyster pudding which came surrounded by mounds of delicious fresh vegetables. Valerie watched him eat this feast with disbelief.

'You won't be able to move!'

'I need energy,' he smugly told her.

'What for? You never seem to do any work!'

'For chasing you,' he said, his hazel eyes wicked, watching her blush and scowl at him, and laughing at her predictable reaction.

The meal made them both sleepy, and they sat over coffee in the bar for far too long, until Valerie caught sight of a clock and groaned. 'It's half-past three now! Come on! Molly will think I'm not coming!'

They reached the farm three-quarters of an hour later, having lost their way in the deep, ancient lanes which led to it through fields of stubble which had lately been harvested and were playing host to flapping hordes of scavenging birds, gulls, crows, magpies who made patterns in black and white as they flew up into the air.

Gib finally asked an old man on a bicycle for directions, and they discovered that they had passed the turning to the farm twice already.

Old gates, propped open by a stone, led into a shady path between thick hedgerows shining with scarlet hips and haws and fat purple blackberries. They saw the farm at a turn in the path, an old house, with thick, plastered walls painted cream, an old, mossy roof, set among trees which protected it from the wind which must blow down the valley from the sea, some ten miles off.

'Perfect place for a peaceful holiday,' Valerie ruefully said. 'And I'm about to ruin it for Molly.'

'How did you come to get her story in the first place?' asked Gib.

'A tip-off from someone in her lawyer's office, and don't ask for a name because you know I have to protect my sources. This one is very useful. I went round to see Molly to check the tip out, and she was so angry with Mac Cameron for refusing to accept that he was the father of the baby that she talked a blue streak, but since the rest of the Press got on to her she's regretting she ever saw me, I suppose.'

'She's trying to make Cameron admit he's the father, and pay an allowance for the child?'

'Yes, she's very bitter about him, and if he is the father she's entitled to support for herself and the baby—but having met her lawyers I know who will get the most money out of the case, and it won't be Molly.'

They pulled up outside the house, tyres scrunching on
the gravel drive, and Molly came out the front door. She
was heavily pregnant, and walked slowly, with dignity,
in her pretty blue smock dress, the sun gleaming on her
long, dark hair, her skin smooth and glowing with health.

Gib whistled softly. 'I can see why Cameron was attracted! She's lovely.'

They got out of the car and Molly looked nervously
at Gib, blinking. 'He isn't a photographer? I don't
want——'

'No, I'm not. I just drove Val down here,' Gib said
quickly, offering his hand. 'Hello, Molly, I'm Gib,
Valerie's boyfriend.'

Valerie went pink and gave him a furious look. How
dared he say that? But Molly relaxed and smiled at him
as she shook hands.

'Does she often have to work at weekends? That must
be boring for you.'

'Yes, it is,' he said, grinning. 'That's why I try to tag
along with her whenever I can, and it has been no
hardship to drive down here to Devon; what lovely
countryside around here!'

Molly smiled back at him. 'Yes, isn't it gorgeous?
Well, come in and have some tea. My cousins are both
out, working around the farm. If you don't mind, we'll
sit in the kitchen to save me time walking backwards and
forwards with tea things.'

They walked through a hall with an old red-flagged
floor, sunk deep with age and gleaming with centuries
of loving polish. Purple Michaelmas daisies and white
and gold chrysanthemums glowed in a great earthen-
ware vase in an empty red-brick hearth.

Gib's appreciative eyes roamed over the cream walls,
the dark paintings of landscapes and family portraits,
as Molly led them through the hall and into the back of

the house to the kitchen which was large, sunny and warm. A spaniel slept next to an old range which was alight and giving out a gentle heat; red and white gingham curtains hung at the windows, whose sills were crammed with red and white geraniums in pots, there was a well-scrubbed deal table with some chairs set round it in the centre of the room, and along one wall a huge dresser loaded with china, some of it looking quite valuable.

'What a lovely room,' Valerie said, gazing around evasively.

'Isn't it nice? I've always loved it here. Sit down and I'll make the tea.'

'Can I help?'

'You could get three cups and saucers down from the top shelf of the dresser. I find it a bit awkward, stretching up there,' Molly said, pointing, as she switched on an electric kettle.

'I'm the tallest, I'll do it,' Gib said, reaching easily to the shelf.

Molly was getting out food, a large fruit cake, scones, sponge fingers dusted with sugar. Valerie eyed it with alarm.

'It's very kind of you, but we only ate an hour ago,' she said. 'I couldn't eat anything.'

Molly looked round, her pink mouth a circle of disappointment. 'Oh...are you sure? I baked all this myself, this morning. I like to do what I can to help Janet and Andy out. Won't you just have a scone? I'm thrilled with the way they came out. My last lot were like stones, but I think I'm getting the mixture right now. These are very light.'

Gib sat down at the table. 'I love scones,' he said. 'Did you make the jam, too?'

It was obviously home-made, in a pot with a hand-written label giving the date on which it was made, but Molly giggled and shook her head.

'Afraid not, this is Janet's strawberry jam, made with their own strawberries, her gooseberry jam, or cherry jam...'

'Made with their own cherries?'

She nodded and Gib grinned. 'I think I'll have that, I love cherry jam.' He took a small plate and a knife, helped himself to one of the scones, and began putting on jam and some of the thick, clotted Devon cream which Molly said was also made on the farm.

Molly made the tea and poured it, gave Valerie a cup and sat down with them, her face sobering again.

'What did you want to ask me, then?'

Valerie glanced at Gib. 'I think we ought to be alone for the interview, don't you?' She was embarrassed by the idea of asking Molly some of the more personal questions about her sex life while Gib was listening.

'Well, if it's going to be very personal, maybe,' Molly said, looking nervous.

'Well, then, after Piggy here has finished eating scones, maybe he'll go for a walk while I talk to you?'

Gib finished a mouthful, said, 'OK,' then smiled at Molly. 'These are great scones, always make them like this.'

She looked pleased. 'Have another one!'

'I don't think I'd better, I've eaten two already!' he said with regret, swallowed some tea and got up. 'Is it OK if I walk around the farmyard?'

'Fine, so long as you don't leave any doors or gates open and let my animals out! Especially the pigs—they cause havoc if they get out!'

He nodded. 'Don't worry, I'll be very careful.'

When he had gone, Valerie got out her notepad and pen, and switched on her recording machine, flatly saying into it, 'Interview with Molly Green in Devon...' and giving the date.

Molly sat tensely, her hands on the table, fingers linked. Valerie looked at her with compunction; the other girl was so pale, her body heavy with the baby she was carrying, and her wide eyes so anxious that it was more difficult to start the interview than it had ever been with any other interview in Valerie's entire career. Normally, she was talking to famous people, often showbusiness people, tough people, who had learnt to wear a hard shell, take anything that was thrown at them. Molly was from another world, she was vulnerable, easily hurt, almost fragile, and Valerie was afraid of upsetting her.

But she had to do her job so she took a deep breath and began. 'Was Mac Cameron the first man you had been to bed with, Molly?'

CHAPTER SIX

'I COULDN'T believe my eyes!' Hazel said on Monday morning when Gina arrived. 'You never said you knew Mac Cameron!'

'You don't understand—I only met him on Saturday night!'

Hazel turned from the filing cabinets, a letter in her hand, her eyes wide. 'He's a fast worker! From that photo I thought the two of you were——'

Pink, Gina said crossly, 'I know! I've seen it. But it isn't true. We had supper after the show, that's all.'

'He didn't take you home?' Hazel seemed quite disappointed.

'He insisted on taking me home, but he did *not* come in, and he didn't even try anything. I thought he might, because his chauffeur was driving—I think Mac has lost his licence, anyway, he said he never drives himself any more. But he didn't lay a finger on me. He didn't even try to talk me into offering him a last cup of coffee. Just said thanks for a lovely evening, and left.'

'What a let-down. I thought he was supposed to be sex-mad and absolutely irresistible,' Hazel said, getting out another couple of letters from the files.

'Maybe it's just his publicity?'

'What about this girl who's supposedly having his baby?'

'Yes,' Gina said slowly. 'Now I've met Mac I'm beginning to have my doubts about her. He just doesn't seem the type to seduce an inexperienced girl of that age, then dump her and refuse to admit he could be the father of her baby.'

Hazel gave her a cynical look. 'No? Or maybe he's a very clever guy who understands women.'

'What does that mean?' Gina demanded, frowning.

'You only spent a couple of hours with him, but he managed to convince you he was as innocent as a lamb, didn't he? Now that's clever, but then he is an actor, and how can you ever really know what they're thinking? After all, pulling the wool over people's eyes is their job!'

Gina looked struck. 'You're right. I hadn't thought of that, but it couldn't all be acting. I'm sure I'd have picked it up if he hadn't been genuine. He was so tolerant, sympathetic, I felt we had a lot in common. And even when that photographer jumped out and took the picture of us Mac just laughed it off.'

'He probably set it up himself.' Hazel came over to her desk and sat down, clipping the file letters into a folder on which she neatly stuck a label she had already printed on her word processor. She was putting together all the information on a technical improvement for the printing works, in readiness for Nick Caspian's return from Stockholm, which was expected some time later that day.

Gina stared at her open-mouthed. 'Why on earth should he?'

'Don't be such a fool, Gina! It wasn't so much the pictures as the caption! He's threatening to sue Nick, and you turn up on a date with him? He was using you against Nick, can't you see that?'

Gina's colour drained away. 'No, I don't believe it. He isn't like that. And, anyway, I'm sure he didn't recognise me. There wasn't the slightest hint that he had.'

'How many times do I have to say it?' Hazel snapped irritably at her. 'He's an actor, for heaven's sake. So he didn't give the slightest hint! Years of training, Gina, that's all.'

'I think I know enough about men——'

Hazel laughed sharply. 'Believe that if you want to! But no woman really knows enough about men. They're a mystery to us. I sometimes think they're aliens, from another planet. We ought to be warned against having anything to do with them, but I suppose we simply prefer having them around to being alone.'

Gina stared at her, taken aback by her tone and the look in her face. It was so unlike Hazel to be bitter. 'Hazel, is something bothering you?'

'Nothing. Why should anything be bothering me?' Hazel muttered, slamming a drawer in her desk shut.

'You're talking in a funny way, not like yourself at all. And you're so pale. You look——'

Hazel interrupted, her voice rising shrilly. 'Don't tell me how I look! I'm just fine, I tell you, there's nothing wrong...'

Gina had never seen her in such a state before and was horrified, especially when Hazel abruptly burst into tears and covered her face with her hands, sobbing.

Gina rushed over to her and knelt beside her chair, putting her arms around her.

'Hazel, whatever is it?'

'Nothing!' Hazel wailed, then muttered in a muffled voice, 'It's just...I think I...but Piet doesn't want...he'll be angry, and I'm scared, Gina, he'll think I did it deliberately, we've quarrelled about it more than once and he'll think I...'

Her voice died away in sobs and Gina hugged her, frowning, trying to unravel the mystery.

'I'm sure Piet would never be really angry with you, whatever you've done. He's mad about you, you know he is! He'd do anything for you.'

Hazel pushed her away and rubbed her hands angrily over her wet face, then said huskily, 'Except let me have a baby!'

Gina drew a startled, comprehending breath. 'Oh. You want to have a baby, and Piet doesn't?'

'Oh, maybe one day,' Hazel said in a defensive voice. 'But not yet, not until——' She broke off, sighing heavily, and Gina frowned, thinking hard.

'Of course, he wants to start up on his own, doesn't he? And he wants you to work with him, and I suppose if you had a baby you'd want to stay home and look after it?'

'I don't know what I'd do! But we could sort something out, get a nanny, maybe get an au pair, or I could take the baby with me to work—I'd at least talk it over with him, argue it out, reach a compromise—but Piet refuses even to do that. He just insisted. No baby. There was no discussion. He told me he didn't even want to talk about it. I wasn't allowed any say in the matter, apparently. He had decided, all by himself, that we wouldn't start a family for a few years, and that was that.'

'Oh, dear,' Gina murmured, not knowing quite what to say.

'He says I'd agreed before we got married that we would wait until we had established our own firm, before we had a baby.' She met Gina's eyes and flared up again, flushing. 'Well, OK, I did, in a way, but...well, the truth is, what really happened was...he said that would be best, and I didn't argue because it seemed so far off, we had just got engaged, I knew it would be ages before we got married, and I didn't really mind much then, having a baby wasn't on my mind, so I just let it slide. I wanted Piet to be happy, I didn't want a disagreement over something that wouldn't matter for ages.'

Gina could understand how that had happened. She remembered how she had let James and her father and Sir George bulldoze her into a marriage for which she hadn't really been prepared. And look at the way Nick Caspian had bullied her into going to California with him! Men could be so insistent and difficult, and most women preferred a quiet life—it was fatally easy to give in to men's demands just to placate and please them.

Hazel sighed. 'But whenever we visited his sister, at Middleburg, and I saw her children, I thought about having a baby of my own and I wanted one more and more, but Piet didn't feel the same way. Whenever I said how lovely it would be he said: "OK, one day, but not for a long time yet, we can't afford it".'

'Well, there isn't any hurry, is there?' Gina said soothingly. 'I mean, you've only just got married, after all. Why not wait a while, a few more months, and just keep dropping little hints, wear him down gradually? I'm sure he'll come round to wanting a baby one day, and there's plenty of time.'

'No,' Hazel said shakily. 'There isn't. Not any more.'

Gina's eyes widened suddenly. 'Hazel! You don't mean you're already...?'

Hazel nodded, tears spurting again. 'Oh, Gina, what am I going to do? My period's late, by a week—I'm never late, always regular as clockwork, what else can it be?'

'It could be any number of things!' Gina protested.

Hazel wasn't listening; she was wiping her eyes with a paper tissue and sniffing. 'Piet is going to be so furious! He's bound to think I did it deliberately. How am I going to tell him?'

Gina gave her an affectionate, wry look. 'Well, before you tell him anything, I suggest you make certain you're pregnant! Get a pregnancy test—it's quite a simple matter. You should have done that at once, you fat-head! At least then you'll know for certain. But personally, I suspect that getting married, and having a lot of worries about living apart from Piet, and travelling to and from Holland all the time, and not being certain about what's going to happen in the future... all that has just upset your routine and made your period late. Also, you've lost a lot of weight lately, much too fast, and that can affect your periods.'

Red-eyed, Hazel said, 'You're so sensible. I hate you.'

Gina laughed. 'Go and wash your face, and put some more make-up on, then you'll feel better. I'll hold the fort until you get back.'

'Thanks,' Hazel said, giving her a watery smile before she left.

The phone on Hazel's desk began ringing a moment later, and Gina leaned over from her own desk to pick it up.

'Mr Caspian's office.'

'Oh, hello, Hazel, this is Sophie Watson, from the legal department. What time is Mr Caspian expected back from Stockholm?'

Gina was trying not to think about Nick's return; she didn't know how he would react to that picture of her and Mac Cameron.

Flatly, she said, 'Hazel is out of the office at the moment, but I know Mr Caspian's plane touches down around noon, then he has a lunch appointment in town, so he won't get back to Barbary Wharf until mid-afternoon.'

'I see, thank you. Will you tell him that Mr Sandel wants to talk to him when he has the time?'

'I'll make sure he gets the message.' Did Henry Sandel want to discuss that photograph of her and Mac Cameron? Gina wondered.

There was a pause, then Sophie asked, 'That isn't Mrs
Tyrrell, is it?'

Gina frowned. 'Yes,' she admitted with faint reluctance.

'Mr Faulkner wants to talk to you, I was going to call
you next. Would you hold on, please? I'll tell him you're
on the line.'

Gina didn't have to wait long before Guy Faulkner's
voice smoothly said, 'Hello, Mrs Tyrrell, Guy Faulkner
here. I wondered if you would have time to see me
today?'

'If this is about the photo of me and Mac Cameron...'

'Well, naturally,' he said with dryness in his tone. 'Mr
Sandel and I were startled, to say the least—we had no
idea you knew him.'

'I didn't,' Gina said, and explained. 'And I'm almost
certain that he didn't know who I was!' she ended.

'Ah, but the difference between almost and certain
can be enormous,' Guy drawled, his voice dry. 'And there
is one thing we can be sure about—whether he knew on
Saturday night or not, he knows now!'

That thought had crossed Gina's mind, too, but she
pointed out, 'If he's seen that newspaper!'

'Actors always make sure they see their publicity,' Guy
said with cynical amusement. 'And if he doesn't sub-
scribe to a cutting agency some friend will mention it.
They always do. Do I gather you haven't heard from
him since this supper party?'

'No!' snapped Gina.

'Well, I've no doubt he'll be on the phone to you
before too long. If he asks you out again, of course it
is up to you whether or not you accept——'

'Thank you,' she said with sarcasm.

Guy carried on as if she hadn't interrupted. 'But if
you do see him, please don't let him discuss anything to

do with the article, or Molly Green, with you. It could prejudice our case if he extracted some damaging remark from you; in fact even the most innocent comment could be dangerous.'

'I'm not stupid, Mr Faulkner!' Gina was darkly flushed and furious. How dared he talk to her as if she were a halfwit?

'I'm sure you aren't, Mrs Tyrrell, but you aren't trained in the law, either, and you may not realise when you are giving something away that could help his side and harm ours.'

Gina had lunch with Roz later that Monday, in the plaza, at Pierre's, the French restaurant which was the chic venue in Barbary Wharf and often fully booked for weeks ahead. Roz had just got back from Paris and was full of news about her father and Irena, and the engagement to Esteban which had been announced while Roz was there. 'The party went on most of the night—it took me forty-eight hours to get over it!'

'Is your father happy with the engagement?' Gina asked, crunching into her crudités, and Roz nodded.

'In a way, yes. He is going to miss Irena, of course—I think he wishes the wedding could be put off for a few years—but he likes Esteban and he's glad she chose a man he respects. I like Esteban, too, but I'm worried about the age-gap—she's so young, and Esteban is quite a few years older, and he's been married before. I think that makes a difference, don't you? I wonder if he isn't rather set in his ways, and less adaptable than a younger man might be? I suppose all we can do is hope it will work out.'

'I think they're rather alike,' Gina slowly said, thinking about it. 'Irena may be young, but she doesn't act young, does she? You'd never guess she was just a student; she can be very solemn.'

'That's true, she can!' agreed Roz, smiling as she finished her grapefruit salad.

'So Esteban plans to move back to Spain after they're married?' Gina had heard that much from Nick, who had already discussed the transfer with Esteban. 'I'm not surprised. It was obvious that he wasn't happy with Nick's change of marketing strategy.' Her mouth twisted grimly. 'When he first came to London, the *Sentinel* was still a serious newspaper, instead of a comic for grown-ups!'

Roz nodded. 'And Esteban is serious-minded, just as solemn as Irena—so maybe you're right, they will make a good pair.'

'I think so. Esteban moved to London because he wanted a change and he admired the *Sentinel*. He didn't realise how much Nick meant to change the paper. Esteban didn't like Nick's plans—he disapproved of the girlie pictures and the *Sentinel* Calendar, the gossip columns, the snatched photos, the hatchet jobs a lot of gossip writers are turning in these days.'

Roz laughed. 'In fact, the whole tone of the paper since it joined Caspian International!'

'I disapprove too!' Gina said fiercely, her green eyes catlike and angry.

Roz made a wry face. 'We all know you do; you never miss a chance to say so!'

'Good! I wish Nick would take as much notice!'

'Oh, I don't think Nick misses anything you do!' Roz said drily, and Gina grimaced, changing colour, her eyes flickering with nerves.

'I hope you're wrong about that! I'm dreading what he may say if he sees that photo of me and Mac!'

'If he does?' Roz repeated, laughing. 'What do you mean, if? You don't really think Nick isn't going to hear about it?'

Gina groaned. 'I suppose that's too much to ask!'

'Much too much!' Roz said, amusement in her eyes and voice.

'Well, he can't eat me!' Gina defiantly shrugged.

'Let's hope he doesn't try, anyway!' said Roz as the waiter arrived with their main course. They had both chosen trout, grilled, with almonds, mangetout and green beans. Roz began delicately filleting her fish, her eyes on the plate as she asked, 'By the way, isn't Hazel well? She snapped my head off this morning when I rang before you got in, and that isn't like her.'

Gina couldn't tell Roz the truth, so she said evasively, 'It isn't easy being married to someone who lives in another country! Talking about marriage, I thought you and Daniel had decided to make it legal?'

'We have, but it isn't easy to fix a date. I only have a small family, Des and Irena...'

'And Esteban, don't forget him!'

Roz laughed. 'Do you know, I had? Yes, and Esteban. It isn't a problem fixing a date when they can all come, but Daniel comes from a big family who live all over France, and it seems they must all come or we shall be outcasts, so we're trying to work out a date suitable for everyone. The farmers are the worst problem—whenever we suggest a date they're going to be busy harvesting, ploughing, lambing, or mending walls! They don't seem to have much free time.'

'Neither do I,' Gina said, looking at her watch and groaning. 'I'll skip the pudding, and just have coffee. I must get back.'

'Before Nick arrives?' grinned Roz, and Gina tried to laugh too, but she wasn't really in the mood for joking about it.

She was very nervous about Nick's reaction to that photo, and as she walked back into her office ten minutes later her mouth was dry.

Hazel looked up and saw her expression, the flick of her eyes towards Nick's door. 'It's OK, he isn't back yet, you can relax!'

'I think I'd rather get it over with. My nerves are in a bad way, waiting for him to get here!' Gina groaned as she sat down behind her desk.

Hazel smiled briefly, still rather pale. She gathered up a pile of folders. 'I'm just going to the legal department with these. I won't be long, hold the fort.'

She had only been gone a few minutes when the phone began to ring on Gina's desk.

'Gina?' The voice was husky, uncertain.

'Yes,' she said, trying to identify the caller in her mind. She was sure she knew the voice, but who was it?

'This is Mac Cameron,' he said flatly, and she bit her lip, realising that she had hoped she would never hear from him again.

'Oh. Hello.'

'So it is you!' Mac muttered, then, 'You lied to me! You didn't tell me who you really were!' he accused in a low, angry voice, but she remembered what Hazel had said, and wondered what he really felt, and if he was just acting.

'You knew!' She deliberately charged her voice with dry scorn, and he reacted fiercely.

'I did not!'

'Then why did you have the photographer come along?'

'I didn't!' he said, sounding so sincere in his fury that she almost believed him. 'Don't bother with any more of these pretences, Gina! What's the point now? I know what you were up to, and it was you who got that guy along to snatch a photo. The photo was part of your plan!'

'Sell a photo to a rival newspaper?' she angrily mocked. 'Now, would we?'

'If it suited your game, yes!' He sounded bitter. 'I've already rung them, to ask who gave them the tip-off, and if it came from you, but they just laughed and said they never revealed their sources. But then they told me to ask you myself, so I knew they were giving me a little hint that I was right, it was you who set it up.'

Gina was silent for a second, frowning. Whatever Hazel said, she couldn't help believing him. He sounded so outraged.

'I really liked you, too,' he said. 'And I'll tell you something even funnier. This will really make you laugh! I very nearly confided in you, I needed to talk to someone sympathetic...but caution stopped me, thank God. I've been caught like that before, said too much to the wrong person and read about it in the gutter Press sooner or later. I know some people say all publicity is good publicity, but I don't like reading about my private feelings in the newspapers. Not when it really matters. I've learnt not to talk about them. That was what you were hoping for, wasn't it? To get me talking about Molly, get my side of the story and print that, and at the same time maybe find out something that could justify the *Sentinel*, and stop me suing them, or help them win the case. Well, congratulations! You should be on the stage, you know. You've missed your vocation—or maybe not? Maybe you like what you do. You certainly pulled the wool over my eyes and I hope Nick Caspian is proud of you!'

The lash of his angry voice made her flinch. Whatever Hazel said, she couldn't believe that this was acting. It was too painful, too real, and his anger and contempt were not pleasant to hear.

'Mac...listen——' she said huskily, but he interrupted angrily.

'No, I don't think I will, thanks! Nobody makes a fool of me twice, not you, or Molly. Now she really took me for a ride, with those great big eyes and sweet smile! She looked as if butter wouldn't melt in her mouth, and all the time——' His voice broke off, she heard him breathing raggedly, then he hoarsely said, 'Something like that isn't easy to get over. It makes you wonder... Hell, are all women liars and cheats?'

'Mac...' she whispered again, shaken by the pain in his voice. Her mind churned with questions and doubts.

If Mac wasn't lying, Molly had to be—yet Valerie had been so sure of her honesty, and nobody could claim that Valerie Knight was easy to fool. Gina didn't know what to think. It was baffling. Mac sounded so...so convincing! At the same time, she kept remembering the photos of Molly spread out on Nick's desk during the discussions with the lawyers. The girl had the most innocent, truthful eyes she had ever seen. But hadn't Mac just said as much? He accused Molly of being a liar and a cheat, in spite of her big eyes and sweet smile. Was he acting his anger, or was Molly the one who was acting?

'Mac, just answer me this——' she began, wanting to ask him if he and Molly had ever been lovers, but he didn't let her finish, his voice curt and fierce.

'Don't waste your breath. I've got nothing more to say! I just rang to tell you what I thought of you and Nick Caspian and your damned newspaper! I'm going ahead with the lawsuit! You've got away with wrecking other people's lives, but you aren't doing that to me and getting away with it. You'll pay through the nose for printing lies about me.'

The phone slammed down and she sat with her receiver in her hand for a long moment, her face pale,
before she slowly replaced it.

Only then did she realise that she was not alone any
more. The door to Nick's office had been closed, but
now it was open, and he stood there watching her. How
long had he been there listening to her talking to Mac
Cameron?

Nick didn't look like a man suffering from travel
weariness after his flight back from Stockholm. He was
immaculate in a dark grey suit and smooth white shirt,
the city uniform of the successful male, yet somehow he
managed to convey an air of physical threat which argued
with those civilised clothes. Was that because Nick was
unsmiling, face hard as flint, his implacable grey eyes
cutting into her in a cold dissection of what she was
feeling?

A shiver ran down her spine at the hostility in his face,
but she tried to sound calm. 'Oh, you're back!' It was
a statement of the obvious, but it was all she could
manage to come up with at that moment.

'Where's Hazel?' was all he replied.

'She took some papers to the lawyers.' Gina wished
Hazel hadn't gone and left her alone. It was clear that
Nick was not in a pleasant mood; he alarmed her when
he looked like that.

'Come in here!' He gave a peremptory gesture, turning
on his heel to stalk back into his office.

She felt more like running in the opposite direction,
but if she did she could be sure he would catch up with
her, and her nerve failed at the thought of what he might
do to her then, so she got up and shakily followed him.

He had taken a seat behind his desk, his broad
shoulders back and his hands laid flat on the leather top.
It was a position of power, taken up quite deliberately—

Nick was sitting in judgement on her, his hard, narrowed eyes like stone as they watched her come towards him and Gina couldn't help trembling although she fought for control of her muscles.

'What the hell is all this about you and Cameron?' The question came so explosively that she flinched and could only stammer.

'I...w...he...'

'Feeling guilty, Gina?' His mouth twisted and she looked away, her lashes cloaking her nervous eyes.

'I've got nothing to feel guilty about!'

Nick's face tightened, he hurled questions at her like knives, sharp and pointed. 'No? How long has it been going on? And if it's so innocent, why didn't you say you knew him? Why let me find out from a snatch picture in another paper? And what the hell do you expect other people to think? You sat in this office and listened to the lawyers and that girl from Features, and Colette Tse, and you knew just how much rode on it, yet you never said you knew Cameron!'

'I only met him this weekend!' she got out in a rush as he paused for breath. 'I went to see his show on Saturday, just out of curiosity, because the weather was bad and I had nothing to do, and I ran into Sir Dermot Gaskell——'

'Gaskell!' erupted Nick.

'Yes, and he took me round back stage to a little party they were having, and I was introduced to him...to Mac.'

Nick's brows were a straight black line above his frowning eyes. 'So it was Gaskell who engineered it.'

'Well, he introduced us, but Sir Dermot doesn't know about the lawsuit, how could he?'

'He knows Cameron,' Nick pointed out bitingly. 'And Gaskell is no friend of mine, either. He wouldn't mind doing me an injury.'

Gina bit her lip, silently admitting that might be true. Sir Dermot did not like Nick.

'All right,' Nick went on curtly, watching her. 'You met Cameron... how did this picture get taken?'

'He asked me to supper, after the show, that's all. It was just bad luck that a photographer happened to get a picture of us!'

'Bad luck?' Nick repeated, his mouth curling. 'Luck had nothing to do with it. That was no opportunist snatching a picture. Whoever took the photograph knew who you were, for a start—and knew Cameron was threatening to sue the *Sentinel*, not to mention the rest.'

Her green eyes were wide and confused. 'The rest?'

'You and me!'

A little flush crept up her face. 'Oh... that...'

'Yes,' Nick snapped. 'That!'

He picked up a copy of the newspaper from the desk in front of him and read the caption aloud in a furious voice, then flicked an icy look at her. 'I suppose you told Cameron you had a "long-running feud" with me?'

'No, I didn't!'

Nick ignored her denial. 'Well, here it is, in black and white. And this friend who's quoted, saying that you're angry with me and that dating Cameron is your way of getting back at me? That would be Cameron himself, would it?'

Her skin burned and she looked away. 'No! I didn't tell him anything! I never mentioned you. I didn't even tell him my surname. He didn't know who I was!'

Nick laughed furiously. 'Sir Dermot Gaskell introduced you, but didn't tell him who you were? Do you really expect me to believe that? I know how formal old Gaskell can be!'

She bit her lip. 'Maybe he is in financial circles, but this was at a party, and he just called me Gina—he didn't

mention my surname. I'm certain Mac didn't know who
I was, and that it wasn't him who tipped off the guy
who snatched that picture. I think someone at the restaurant did that, someone who recognised both me and
Mac, and the photographer was a freelance. It must have
been the newspaper who came up with the story about
a possible lawsuit.' She drew breath, not daring to meet
his eyes. 'And ... and that stuff about ... about you and
me ...'

'Yes, what about it?' Nick tersely demanded.

'Well,' she stammered. 'You know how newspaper
people gossip, Fleet Street is a small world, lots of your
reporters have worked elsewhere and keep up with
friends. Gossip spreads like wildfire.'

'Then why feed it?' Nick bitterly asked her. 'Why do
you keep arguing with me, sniping at me, fighting me,
in public? If there's gossip it is because you give people
something to talk about.'

'You know why I fight you!' she said huskily. 'I'm
fighting for something I believe in, something I love! I
don't like what you're doing to the *Sentinel*, and I won't
pretend I do, or give in to you the way everyone else
does.'

He sat behind his desk, his face taut and dark with
temper, staring at her. 'Well, at least promise not to see
Cameron again!'

'I doubt if he'll want to see me,' she said wryly. 'He
was very angry when he saw the paper and discovered
who I was! He thought I was trying to trick him
somehow. That's why I'm sure it really wasn't him who
tipped them off.'

'I don't give a damn whether it was him or not!'
Nick snarled. 'You're not to see him again, do you
understand?'

Gina decided it might be wiser not to argue with him, but at the back of her mind she knew that if Mac ever relented towards her she would jump at the chance to see him again. He had left her with a lot of unanswered questions in her head, and she wanted to know the answers to them.

CHAPTER SEVEN

VALERIE spent most of that Monday morning doing an interview at the Savoy with an American ballet dancer who was bringing his all-black company over to Britain for a long tour. He was easy to talk to, naturally witty and quick with a phrase, he gave her any number of quotes and made some points which would be controversial. They would undoubtedly get a lot of letters from some of the things he said, and Valerie was excited— this was going to be a good interview. The photographer arrived just as she was finishing, and she left him in the dancer's suite to get a series of shots to go with her article.

'Thanks very much, I enjoyed meeting you, Aloysius,' she said as she left and the black dancer gave her a graceful wave, but she saw that he was already turning his mind to being photographed. He would make an amazing subject on film; that lithe, silky body of his seemed able to take up any pose and hold it without strain for as long as necessary. He had told her that was due to training and exercise, but obviously it had been a natural talent, to begin with, which he had refined with hard work.

She had another interview lined up for that afternoon, but she went back to Barbary Wharf to start writing up the interview with the dancer before she snatched a quick lunch.

Today it was very sunny, but not hot. The sky was as clear as blue glass, not a cloud in sight; but there was a chill on the air and as she walked across the plaza she saw russet leaves blowing along the embankment. Autumn was not far away.

Colette noticed her the minute she walked on to the editorial floor, caught her eye and beckoned.

'I was coming in, anyway,' Valerie assured her, closing the door behind her. She sensed a battery of eyes fixed on her back as she took the chair opposite Colette's desk. The trouble with open planning was that, even if they couldn't hear what was said inside this glass-walled box which was Colette's office, everyone could see them.

By now, many people had probably heard some whisper about the threat of a lawsuit, and everyone in Editorial was thinking, thank heavens it wasn't me! Nobody liked being caught in a legal tangle; it could mean the end of your job if the paper lost money.

'Well? What did you find out from Molly Green?' Colette was in one of her crisp moods, which meant she was busy and in no mood to waste words.

'I talked to her for hours, and she stuck to her story. We went over it again and again, and you know I still believe her! I didn't get a hint of a lie, anywhere. She swears she never slept with anyone else, either before or after she met Cameron—he was the first, and she's still in love with him.' She looked at Colette, grimacing. 'Can you beat that? The guy treats her like this, but she still loves him?'

'She told you that?'

'Yes. I asked, and she didn't answer for a minute, but I saw it in her eyes. She's crazy about him, even now, and she's hurting badly. I don't think she's sleeping very well; she's unhappy. I felt a heel for badgering her, but I had to keep nagging at her to make sure I was getting the truth this time. So I asked her again, ''Are you still in love with him?'' and then she told me. She wishes she could hate him, but she can't. She doesn't understand why he's lying, she said, or refusing to admit it's his baby, and she knows her mother and father are right, and he doesn't love her, after all, he'd just been using her ... but she can't stop loving him.' Valerie ran a hand over her blonde hair, groaning angrily. 'Men! All the trouble in the world starts with them!'

Colette laughed. 'And most of the pleasure, too.'

'But is it worth it when they dump you and go off with someone else?' Valerie grimly asked. 'Especially if they leave you literally to hold the baby, like Molly?'

Colette shrugged. 'That never happened to me. I made sure of that. Why didn't she? I wonder, did she deliberately get pregnant to get him to marry her? Is that why he refuses to admit it is his baby?' She thought about that, chin in hand, then turned businesslike again, and nodded. 'Well, whatever—we stay with her, and back our story. OK?'

Valerie gave her a grateful smile. 'Yes, fine, thank you, Colette.'

'You had better be right,' Colette told her drily. 'Now, let's say you are, and she *is* telling the truth. So where does that leave us? It must be Cameron who's lying, in that case—and if he is he won't be able to prove he isn't the father. Those photos tell their own story. She was with him on that yacht, and they were very intimate. You know, I don't believe he'll bring this suit. He's trying to put the fear of hell into us, hoping to frighten us into publishing an apology. If we backed off, it might weigh with the courts when Valerie brings a paternity case against him. These things take years to come to court, anyway. By the time it does, she'll have had the baby and we can have a blood-test to make sure Cameron could be the father. Unfortunately it won't prove that he is, of course. Only that he could be.'

The telephone on her desk rang and she picked it up. 'Features editor. Yes? Oh, yes, she's here. I'll send her along to you at once.'

Colette put the phone down and gave Valerie a wry look. 'That was Guy Faulkner; he wants to hear what happened when you visited Molly Green.'

Valerie pulled a face. 'He gave me a list of very personal questions to ask her. I hated having to ask them, but I did.' She grinned at Colette. 'But he asked me out to lunch!'

'Go!' urged Colette. 'He could be a useful friend to have! Lawyers always are.'

'Cynic!' Valerie got up. 'Anything else you wanted to talk about?'

Colette shook her head. 'I think we've covered everything. Get along to Legal.'

Then, as Valerie was going out, she added, 'Don't forget to have the interview with Aloysius Jackson on my desk before five this afternoon, will you?'

Valerie grimaced but nodded. She always complained when she was kept busy, or given a deadline by which to finish a job, but at the same time it was satisfying to have the adrenalin flowing through her body, as it did whenever she was working at top speed.

She popped into the ladies' before going to the legal department. It only took two minutes to run a brush lightly over her blonde hair, deftly renew her lipstick, check on the seams of her smooth-fitting stockings, and she wanted to look her best before she saw Guy Faulkner.

She was wearing a carnation-pink silk shirt tucked into a white skirt which showed a great deal of her long, slim legs. The outfit had been getting attention ever since she left her flat that morning and when she walked into Guy Faulkner's office his reaction was just as flattering.

'Hello!' He got to his feet and came round his desk, looking at her with open interest. 'Thanks for coming to see me.' He pulled back a chair and she sat down, crossing her legs while he watched. He took a perch on the edge of his desk, close beside her. 'So how did you get on with Molly Green?'

Valerie told him what she had told Colette, and he listened intently, bending towards her and nodding.

'You're totally sold on her story, then?'

'Absolutely,' Valerie insisted, her violet-blue eyes raised towards him and wide with sincerity.

He gazed into them. 'Well, then, we must wait and see if Mac Cameron means to go ahead with the case.'

'And it will take years to come to court?'

He shrugged. 'Possibly. The courts are very congested, cases can take some years to reach the top of the list. When is this baby due?'

'Next month. Then we can have a blood-test to check if it could be his baby.'

'And if the test is positive, we'll be in a much stronger position,' Guy agreed, looking at his watch. 'Nearly twelve. What are you doing for lunch?'

'I was going to grab a snack from Torelli's and eat in the office,' she said.

'Will you have lunch with me instead?'

'Thanks, I'd like that,' Valerie said.

'Good.' Guy smiled at her, then leaned over and dialled Pierre's number. 'Hello, Guy Faulkner here—any chance of a table for two?' He grimaced, listening to the reply. 'OK, thanks.'

'Fully booked?' guessed Valerie and he nodded.

'How do you feel about Chinese? We could eat across the road at the Hong Wah, you can usually get a table there.'

'And they're faster than Pierre's,' Valerie said, so Guy rang and this time was able to book a table.

As they were leaving the office Sophie came in with a sheaf of documents in her hand. She flicked a cold look at Valerie, who gave her a bland smile.

'Hello, Sophie, how are you?'

'Fine,' Sophie said offhandedly. 'Guy, these are the Whittaker papers—you said you wanted them urgently.'

He frowned. 'Yes, put them on my desk, I'll deal with them after lunch. I should be back by half-past one. We're lunching across the road, at the Hong Wah.'

Sophie gave Valerie a quick, sharp look, and Valerie gazed coolly back. Was Sophie pleased to hear she was dating Guy, instead of Gib? If she was, she hid her feelings, her face emptying of all expression in a second. No doubt she had learnt that trick in working here? Lawyers had a lot in common with actors; it was not easy to tell what they were thinking.

But as Valerie and Guy walked away Valerie felt the other girl's hostility like a knife in her back. Just how serious was Sophie about Gib? she wondered bleakly. She would have felt sorry for her if it weren't for her own tangled feelings about Gib, and admitting that was depressing.

'Cheer up!' Guy said as they crossed the plaza towards the Silver Street exit. 'Forget the court case, and enjoy your lunch. Life is too short to waste any of it worrying over something that may never happen.'

It was good advice, and Valerie took it, smiling back at him. In fact, the food was excellent and all freshly cooked. There was a fixed meal available at a very good price, so they both had that—crab soup, a beautifully flavoured clear broth with crabmeat lightly cooked in it, followed by huge prawns cooked with tomatoes, a touch of garlic and spring onions, served with boiled rice and steamed mixed vegetables.

They decided to have China tea with it, instead of wine, as both of them had a busy afternoon ahead of them and wanted to keep their heads clear.

Guy was a good companion—he made her laugh and asked intelligent questions about her job. When she asked him about his work he was just as intelligent and funny in his replies, and apparently very frank; she felt she had learnt a lot about him as well as his job.

'We must do this again, soon,' he said as they walked back across the plaza, and Valerie smiled back at him.

'I'd love to!' she agreed, watching Mrs Torelli, who was sweeping leaves from in front of her snack bar, or, rather, was leaning on the broom with which she had been sweeping, and watching the passers-by with small black, curious eyes.

There was a queue of customers inside the snack bar, waiting for Roberto Torelli to serve them. One turned his head to stare, and Valerie coloured, looking away without meeting his narrowed eyes. Trust Gilbey Collingwood to see her with Guy! He never missed a thing, did he?

She looked hurriedly at her watch and made a face. 'I'd better grab a taxi. I've got an appointment at Kensington at two. At this time of day, it will take half an hour to get there, and it's almost half-past one. Thanks for lunch, Guy—see you.'

He grinned at her as she rushed away, a headlong flight across the stone paving of the plaza, as if the hounds of hell were on her trail, and Valerie felt as edgy as if they were! She wanted to get into a taxi before Gib caught up with her, and she was certain he would be coming to look for her.

She dived through the gate into North Street, where she should find a taxi on the rank. It wasn't worth driving her car around London—finding somewhere to park was a nightmare during the day. She usually left her car at home and used public transport, but now that she was late she would have to take a taxi and argue her case when she put in her expenses sheet.

Reaching the pavement, she stopped in her tracks. There were no taxis waiting on the rank. As she stood there, biting her lip, she heard running footsteps behind her, and her nerves leapt fiercely.

She turned to face him like an animal at bay, and Gib halted in front of her, his eyes glittering angrily.

'So you are dating Faulkner!'

She didn't answer that. Instead, she attacked him in turn. 'I thought you weren't working today!'

'I came in to help out for a morning because someone was taken sick and they were short-handed in the office, but the panic is over now, and I'm not needed any more.' He looked down at her, scowling. 'And don't change the subject! Are you going to be seeing Faulkner again?'

'As he works in the same building I'd say that was likely, wouldn't you?' she sarcastically retorted, tossing back her blonde hair in an irritated gesture.

'You know what I meant! Are you going out with him again?'

'If I want to, I certainly shan't ask your permission, anyway!' Valerie refused to let him force her on to the defensive. 'Who do you think you are? Cross-examining me...bullying me...'

'I've never bullied you!' he denied sharply, his brows drawn together. 'Although, I have to admit, I've wanted to give you a good slap often enough, but I was brought up not to hit women, even if they soundly deserve it!'

'You had better not, either!' she threatened, and saw his hazel eyes leap.

'Don't provoke me, Valerie,' he said in soft menace, and her mouth went dry.

He took a step nearer, and she backed, only to find herself in a corner of the wall surrounding the Barbary Wharf complex. Before she could slide out again Gib blocked her way, his powerful body planted right in front of her and his hands on the wall on either side, his arms imprisoning her.

Her heart began crashing into her ribs and she trembled helplessly. He was much too close, and her head was swimming. She looked up to protest and couldn't get a word out. The way he was looking at her seriously undermined her defences.

'I don't want you going out with other men, Valerie,' he murmured with an arrogance that took her breath away. 'Understand?'

Valerie didn't understand anything, least of all herself; she only knew that every time she saw Gib she began losing control, and that terrified her. She had to get away from him before he saw the helplessness in her eyes.

With wild relief she saw a taxi pulling into the rank behind them. 'I've got to go,' she muttered, edging sideways. 'I'm doing an interview in fifteen minutes! I can't be late.'

'Promise not to date Faulkner again and you can go!' Gib was implacable, his face hard and determined.

'Oh, OK, I promise!' she said. 'Just let me go!'

He caught her face between his hands and bent his head to take her mouth possessively. Deep inside her a pulsating heat throbbed, and she forgot everything else, kissing him back, her eyes closed.

Gib lifted his head, staring down at her in satisfaction. 'Stop fighting it, Valerie. You're mine and you
know it.'

She was weak-kneed, shivering. In a shaky, dazed voice
she said, 'I must go...' and, smiling, he stood out of
her way. She made it somehow to the taxi, her legs almost
giving under her, opened the door and gave the driver
the address in Kensington. By the time they were driving
away she had pulled herself together a little, and she was
angry because it had taken him no time at all to get to
her.

She leaned out of the taxi window and called back to
Gib, 'You blackmailed that promise out of me, so it
doesn't count, anyway!'

She just had time to catch the black rage which flared
into his face, then the taxi had turned the corner and he
was out of sight, but Valerie couldn't get the memory
of Gib's expression out of her head for the rest of that
day.

She pulled herself together and concentrated on her
interview, then went back to the office to write the article
on the all-black ballet company which was beginning its
tour of Britain. It wasn't easy to work. She couldn't stop
thinking about Gib and every time she did her heart
turned over violently and she couldn't breathe.

She was dangerously close to falling in love with him,
and that would be folly! she told herself crossly!

Then, like a bolt of lightning from a blue sky, the
truth hit her, and she sat staring at nothing with a dazed
expression on her face. It was too late to tell herself not
to fall in love with Gib. She *was* in love with him! It had
happened long ago, although she had been refusing to
admit it, and every time she saw him it got worse; she
wanted him more desperately. How could she have been
so blind?

'Stuck for inspiration?' another reporter asked as he walked past, and grinned. 'Try banging your head on the wall. It works for me, every time.'

Valerie forced a grin in reply. 'I wondered why your brains were addled, John.'

She couldn't sit here where everyone could see her; she had to be alone. She went out, to the ladies' cloakroom, which was empty, luckily, sat down on one of the small white chairs and tried to think, but the clutch of sensuality kept getting in the way. Every time she thought of Gib her stomach contracted, she went weak with desire, her mind swamped by images of him smiling at her, touching her, kissing her.

The door opened and she hurriedly jumped up, managing a smile as another girl came into the room. Pretending to be tidying her hair, Valerie checked on her reflection in the mirror, amazed to find how normal she looked. Why didn't it show in her face, this turmoil of feeling? Only her eyes gave anything away, their blue darkened with emotion, the pupils dilated and glistening, black as olives. She turned away sharply, and went back to work.

When Gina arrived on Tuesday morning she was surprised to find that Hazel wasn't at her desk. Usually Hazel was the first one there!

Gina began going through her in-tray to see if anything was urgent, but within two minutes the phone was ringing, and for the next half-hour it barely stopped. Nick wasn't in yet, and she had to keep fielding enquiries meant for him, and some of the junior secretaries kept coming in to consult Hazel about that day's work. It was a hectic start to the day.

At nine-thirty Hazel finally arrived, so pale and drawn that Gina immediately realised what she was going to say before she opened her mouth and said it.

Gina said it for her, getting up. 'The test was positive?'

Hazel nodded, close to tears.

Gina hugged her. 'Don't look like that, you'll have me in tears in a minute! It will be OK, Hazel! I know Piet didn't want a baby yet, but he'll come round to the idea, now it's actually going to happen. Sit down and have a cup of coffee. I just made a fresh pot.'

Hazel sat down behind her desk while Gina poured the coffee. 'My doctor asked if I wanted an abortion,' she said flatly as Gina handed her the cup.

Green eyes horrified, Gina stared but was careful not to comment. 'What did you say?'

Hazel laughed bleakly. 'That I'd think about it. He said I shouldn't wait too long. It's best to get it over with as soon as possible, the earlier the better.'

Gina bit her lip. 'The first thing to do is talk to Piet...'

'I don't have to tell him at all. I could go in and have it done and be back at work in a couple of days, according to the doctor. Then Piet need never know.'

Gina was appalled. 'Hazel, you can't! This is Piet's baby, too, and he has a right to be involved in choosing what happens to it. Look, if Piet wanted it, you would want it too, wouldn't you?'

Hazel's eyes blurred with tears. 'Of course I would! But...'

'Maybe he won't want it, but you can't be sure about that. You really must tell him and talk it over; you can't make such an important decision without even consulting him! Look, if you need to go over to Utrecht and talk to him——'

'No,' Hazel decided in a less strained voice, running a hand over her wet eyes. 'No, I'll talk to him at the weekend. You're right, I'm being pessimistic. Maybe Piet will feel differently now.' She gave Gina a crooked smile. 'Thanks. It really helps to have someone to talk to who understands. I can't talk to my mother, she would be shocked.'

In the middle of that week, Gina and Nick Caspian and the rest of the managerial team flew from Heathrow to San Francisco—a long and tiring journey which left Gina with jet lag, feeling limp and drained. She leaned back in the corner of the limousine taking them into the city, her eyes shut. 'How far is it now?'

'Sixteen miles,' Nick said. He had sent the other four executives in the second limousine which had met them at the airport because they were going to different destinations. He and Gina would be staying with his mother, in her home, while the other men would be staying at the St Francis Hotel in Powell Street, downtown in San Francisco.

'That far?' she said in dismay. 'Really? I was hoping I could go to bed and get some real sleep. I didn't sleep on the plane, just dozed.'

'That isn't a good idea. You have to adjust your body clock to this time zone; you must stay up until everyone here is going to bed, then you'll wake up tomorrow feeling much better.'

She groaned. 'I don't believe I'll ever feel better. My head is banging like a drum and I feel faintly queasy. I just want to lie down somewhere quiet.'

'Poor Gina!' Nick said, then she felt his arm go round her. Her eyes flew open in alarm in time to see the world dizzyingly tilt and slide down.

But it wasn't the world tilting, it was her, she was falling. For a second she didn't realise what was happening, then she found herself lying across the seat, her head on his knees.

'What on earth——?' she began chokingly, staring up at his shadowed face in the back of the limousine, and Nick put a long, tanned finger on her lips, silencing her.

'Shut your eyes again and just lie still. You won't get any sleep, but a rest won't hurt you. In this traffic it will take us an hour to get to my mother's house.'

'What on earth will the chauffeur think?' she muttered furiously, her mouth moving under his finger, the tickling sensation making her shiver.

'He isn't paid to think,' Nick arrogantly told her, and she wondered what the chauffeur thought of *that* if he heard it!

He was holding her down with one hand pressing into her shoulder, and she wriggled uneasily, aware that her skirt had ridden up, revealing her legs right up to her thighs.

'Let me get up, Nick!' she said, brushing her skirt down again while he watched with amusement.

Stroking a long strand of glowing russet hair back from her hot cheek, he grinned mockingly at her. 'Don't be childish. Why not admit that's much more comfortable than sitting up while we jolt at a snail's pace through a traffic jam?'

Gina decided it was too undignified to go on arguing and struggling with him. She shut her angry green eyes without another word and settled down to try to rest, and he was right—it was more comfortable. In fact, she was almost asleep by the time they finally arrived at Mrs Caspian's house.

'We're here,' Nick said, helping her to sit up, and Gina yawned and blinked sleepily out of the window as the limousine began making its way up a narrow, winding driveway set on a steep hill, between palm trees. Through the fretted, swaying branches of the palms, she caught glimpses of green lawns, shrubs, and up above them a huge Victorian house of gothic design, strangely mysterious seen through the exotic palms.

'The Tower and Cupolas of the Seven Winds,' Nick murmured, and she gave him a startled look.

'What?'

'That is the name of the house. It was set on this hill to be seen from as far away as possible—down there is the bay...' He turned and pointed back behind them. 'You can even see it from there when there's no smog!'

Gina caught the sheen of blue through an opalescent mist which sheathed the distance.

'Was it your mother who chose that name?' she asked, looking back as the limousine swept over the gravel and drew up outside the house.

'No, the man who built the house chose it; he was a romantic.'

Nick sounded cynical, disparaging, his mouth twisting as he spoke.

'I must be, too,' said Gina. 'Because I love the name. And it suits the house.'

The chauffeur opened the door, and Gina climbed out and stood on the drive, staring up at the façade. It was extraordinary—the dominant feature that struck you was a three-storey tower capped by a blue-slate circular roof like a witch's hat, but there were two small, weathered, greenish-bronze-covered domes at the back of the building. Along the first floor of the main body of the house ran a line of tall, high windows each with a beautiful ironwork balcony, painted black, in front of it. A vast porch projected out from the façade. You entered through a high black oak double door which opened as Gina stared at it. A woman appeared, framed in the doorway; thin and elegant in black with a white lace collar, her face remote beneath her silvery, perfectly coiffeured hair.

Gina had a qualm of doubt, of anxiety—would she be welcomed here, in Nick's home, or was she about to be treated with distant hostility?

She wished she had not come.

CHAPTER EIGHT

NERVOUSLY, Gina followed Nick towards the open door and the waiting figure, but as they reached her the silver-haired woman said, 'Welcome back, sir. I hope you had a good flight.'

So this wasn't his mother? Gina thought as Nick introduced her. 'Gina, Mrs Grant is my mother's secretary. This is Mrs Tyrrell, Mrs Grant. She's very tired and would like to go straight to her room. I'll go and see my mother first, though.'

They walked through the marble-floored porch and met a short, dark-haired muscular man of around fifty, in a neat, dark suit and white shirt. Nick greeted him cheerfully. '*Cómo está usted, José*?'

'*Bien, gracias, Señor Nicholas!*' beamed the other, and then asked a long string of rapid questions in Spanish which Gina did not know enough of the language to grasp. Nick answered just as fluently, and then turned to her.

'Gina, this is José—he and his wife, Conchita, have run this house for my mother for twenty years.'

Gina looked into the smiling, dark eyes and shook hands, liking José instantly. There was warmth and strength and a great kindness in his face.

'I hope you will enjoy your visit to San Francisco,' he said.

'I am sure I will. I can't wait to do some sight-seeing and ride on a tram.'

Mrs Grant had moved on into the house and, after a brief chat with José, Nick and Gina followed. Gina caught her breath in disbelief as she found herself in a Victorian gothic version of a medieval baronial hall, enormous, shadowy, with a high beamed roof, a huge stone fireplace with an iron fire-basket in which was piled real logs ready for kindling, a massive oak table running down the centre of the room, and suits of armour standing around the oak-panelled walls, on which hung swords and pikes, crossbows, shields and embroidered banners which looked very old.

'Is all that genuine?' she asked Nick, who gave her an amused look.

'It had better be. It cost my father a fortune. He had people scouring Europe for medieval armour and weaponry for years, and he built up a huge collection, most of which went to a museum when he died. It was one of his hobbies as he got older; he was fascinated by the Middle Ages in Europe, particularly the history of the German states and the East Europeans. He tried to get me to take an interest, but I found it all confusing. That was why he gave his collection away, all except what hangs on these walls. He left this house, and everything in it, to my mother, although she is no more interested in armour than I am.'

'Sir George collected furniture and paintings,' Gina said, rather oppressed by all the weapons of war around her. 'I inherited some of them, I've got them in my flat, but he left some pieces to friends, and others went to a museum, too. Collecting is a sort of obsession, isn't it, once it takes hold of people?'

'My father had been very poor when he was young, so he was obsessed with owning things,' Nick agreed, his face sombre. 'He bought houses and companies, furniture and art, as well as his medieval weaponry. All his homes were stuffed with valuable objects, but once he had acquired them I doubt if he ever really looked at them again. He was always too busy working. With him, it was more the thrill of the chase, hunting down something priceless, beating all opposition to get it. Once he had it, he no longer seemed to care.'

Gina watched him, her green eyes alert to the changing expressions of his face. 'You inherit some of that, don't you?'

He shot her a frowning look. 'What?'

'You love to target a new newspaper group, and you're prepared to do anything to get control; it's the same sort of obsession.'

'No,' he said sharply. 'It isn't the same. It isn't an obsession, I'm not the obsessive type—it's a business strategy, something very different. When I've acquired a company, I don't just forget about it and look for the next target. Caspian International is made up of many different groups within the parent body. As I acquire a new company in a new country I take a lot of trouble to knit it into the existing corporation, which means a lot of travel, endless paperwork, talking on the phone, having meetings . . .'

She already knew that, from working with him throughout the last year. You couldn't deny how hard he worked or how good he was at running the multinational corporation; he had fitted himself for the task by learning to speak most of the major European languages, and he had advised Gina to do the same. She did speak several languages, but she was busy taking lessons in several others at the moment.

Nick was still talking as they walked through the hall. 'I keep my eye on each separate strand of the corporation, and very little escapes me.'

He glanced down at her sideways, his grey eyes glittering, and she flushed, picking up the hidden meanings. She had been one of Nick's targets for a long time, and he wasn't giving up; he was determined not to let her escape. She thought back over everything that had happened that year—he might claim that he was not the obsessive type but how else did you explain the way he had pursued her, even to the extent of moving in next door to keep an eye on her all the time?

Nick halted at the foot of a highly polished, elaborately carved oak staircase which led up to a wide landing dominated by another suit of armour, from which branching flights of stairs led up to the next floor. Mrs Grant had tired of waiting for them and was on the way upwards, her elegant, straight back managing to convey impatience.

Nick shot a look up at her, his mouth curling. 'As you'll find out, my mother's secretary is very efficient and dislikes waste of time,' he whispered to Gina. 'We had better catch up with her.'

When they reached the next floor Mrs Grant was waiting there. 'I'll see you later,' Nick said to Gina. 'Don't fall asleep—take a bath and change; that will make you feel better. I'll see you downstairs in a couple of hours, and we'll go for a short tour of the city—see the usual sights, the Golden Gate Bridge, Chinatown, Fisherman's Wharf. But we'll have to get back here by six. We're having dinner tonight with a number of wholesalers, at the Portman Grill. If I weren't staying here with my mother, the Portman is where I'd stay; it's one of the best hotels I know, and their grill room is superb. I'm sure it will be a memorable evening, and I'd like you to wear something special. I want you to dazzle our company tonight. So if you need any pressing done, just ask Conchita. Mrs Grant will explain the internal telephone system.'

Gina followed Mrs Grant along the long, wide upper hall, on one side of which were arched windows filled with brilliant stained glass, reminiscent of the great cathedrals of France or England, the light filtering through scarlet and jade-green and kingfisher-blue, making rainbow patterns on the magnolia-painted wall on the other side of them. Gina didn't have time to work out which biblical story was represented in each, but she made a quick guess about the second, not a difficult task since a large ark took up pride of place in it, and overhead a dove flew with a leafy twig in its mouth.

Noticing her interest, Mrs Grant said in her clear, cold voice, 'The glass was made in France, of course.'

'In the nineteenth century?'

Mrs Grant nodded.

'When was the house actually built?' Gina asked.

'1907, but it replaced an earlier identical house which was destroyed in the great earthquake of 1906. They were both designed by an extraordinary man, Nathaniel Horner, who had wished to be an artist when he was young but instead was forced to go into his father's shipping business. He was a Sunday painter, throughout his life, but I think his real genius went into designing this house in the later years of his life. He died shortly after moving into it.' Mrs Grant opened a door and politely ushered Gina into a large sunlit room. 'Mrs Caspian chose this room for you. I hope you will be comfortable. It has a good view of the city.'

Gina walked over to the window and looked out. 'It's breathtaking!' she murmured, staring down across the city, a panoramic sweep of roofs and spires and towers down to the gleam of blue water which she knew marked the famous bay area of San Francisco.

Briskly Mrs Grant showed her the rest of the room. 'Your personal bathroom is through that door. In the headboard of your bed, you'll find the control panel for the room—this switch operates the TV, turns it on and off, these deal with the lights, this is the radio switch. This printed card gives the numbers of the internal telephone—my office, the housekeeper's room, the garage, the kitchen, and so on. I suggest that if you should want anything you ring either myself, or Conchita, the housekeeper.'

Gina nodded, suppressing a yawn with difficulty and hoping the older woman hadn't noticed. Mrs Grant overawed her.

'Perhaps you would like some ''English'' tea before you take your bath, for instance?' Mrs Grant suggested.

'I would love some!'

'Earl Grey? Ceylon?'

'Ceylon, thank you,' Gina said, after a hesitation. Earl Grey's faintly scented taste did not quite suit her mood, she decided. The delicate flavour of Ceylon tea was more appealing.

'I'll see to that now,' Mrs Grant said, going towards the door just as José arrived with Gina's luggage. He gave her a friendly smile as he lifted the case on to a luggage rack at the end of her large four-poster bed.

'Would you like help with unpacking? I'll send Conchita up with the tea; she'll be glad to do it,' Mrs Grant said. 'And then she can take away the dress you plan to wear for dinner tonight, and press it for you.'

She didn't wait for Gina to answer; she vanished as she said the last words, and José followed her.

Before he closed the door, he said, 'If there is anything I can do for you, Mrs Tyrrell, dial 14.'

'Thank you.'

Gina was relieved to be alone, to let peace and silence lap around her. She was tired of having to smile politely, make small talk with strangers. The effort took too much energy and she had very little left at the moment. She sat down on a carved oak William Morris style chair by the window and stared out over the city until she was startled by a knock on the door.

This time it was her tea, made in a silver teapot, with matching sugar bowl and cream jug, brought up on a silver tray, by Conchita, the housekeeper, who was a plump, dark-eyed woman of about forty, in a black dress with a lace collar, oddly similar to the one worn by Mrs Grant. Was it some sort of uniform? wondered Gina, smiling at her.

'Thank you, that looks wonderful. And the china is Wedgwood, isn't it? I recognise the pattern, one of their classic styles.'

'*Si, señora!*' the other woman said, with a strong Spanish—or was it Mexican?—accent, nodding, and went on in Spanish, then stopped, seeing Gina's frown of confusion. 'Ah, *no entiende?* I want to say... you are English, so I use English tea service. Mrs Caspian ... she has cabinets full of china, many, many china, from all over the world.'

'That was very thoughtful,' Gina said, touched. Was china something else Zachariah Caspian had collected?

'*Encantado, señora.*'

Gina knew that word—it meant delighted, or enchanted, didn't it?

'*Limón?*' enquired Conchita, and that was easy, too.

'Yes, lemon, thank you.'

Conchita poured a cup of tea, handed it to Gina, saying, 'English biscuits, *señora?*' She beamed happily, placing a plate of very familiar biscuits beside Gina, who managed to show enthusiasm.

'Oh, lovely! How kind!' She gratefully drank the tea, nibbling a ginger biscuit from time to time. She was not hungry, but she didn't want to disappoint Conchita after the other woman had taken so much trouble to please her.

By the time she had finished her tea Conchita had finished hanging up her clothes. She took away over her arm the peacock-blue silk cocktail dress Gina had decided to wear that evening, and deftly carried in her other hand the tea-tray.

Gina bolted the door behind her and stripped, then put on a short green towelling robe and went into the bathroom.

Ten minutes later she lay in a warm, rose-scented bath with her eyes half closed, dreamily contemplating her pink toes as they showed through the water at the far end. The bathroom was utterly modern, yet looked Victorian—clever reproduction, she realised, with hand-painted trails of ivy, rosebuds and full-blown peonies on the white bath and other units, walls painted duck-egg blue, deep-pile carpet in snowy white, solid mahogany cabinets with brass handles. The water ran hot, there were rows of expensive toiletries arranged on shelves behind the bath, and she had poured liberal amounts of rose bath oil into the water before she climbed in with a sigh of pleasure.

This was pure bliss, only marred by the questions buzzing around inside her head like wasps, irritating, stinging, disturbing.

What had Nick said to his mother about her; what did Mrs Caspian know about the *Sentinel* acquisition and the subsequent conflict? About the battles Gina and Nick had fought out for months? Most importantly of all, when was she going to meet Mrs Caspian? And how did Mrs Caspian feel about her?

It was nearly two hours later when she tentatively emerged from her room again, in an amber cotton shift dress, and made her way back downstairs, this time managing to take a closer look at the stained glass windows, identifying Jonah and the whale and Job under his vine as well as Noah's Ark.

Nick came to the foot of the stairs as she arrived, holding up one arm and tapping his wrist-watch. 'I was just coming to look for you! You're fifteen minutes late! Come on, or there won't be time to do some sight-seeing before we have to meet these wholesalers.'

'When am I going to meet your mother?'

'When we get back, she'll have a drink with us before we leave for the Portman.'

The chauffeur-driven limousine was waiting on the drive. 'Is this hired for our stay here, or is it your mother's car?' Gina asked, as she slid into the back of it.

'It's my mother's car. The chauffeur is Ruy, José's eldest son. When my mother's previous chauffeur retired after working for her for years, Ruy applied for the job. We were all surprised because he was training to be a garage mechanic, but in fact he seems to like working in the house, near his family. I think he looks on this house as his home; he has lived here most of his life, of course, and now he plans to marry in the spring, and my mother has given him the little flat over the garage.'

'They must like working for her, to stay for so many years,' Gina thought aloud. It seemed a favourable indication of Mrs Caspian's character that she kept her staff for so long.

Her gaze drifted sideways, towards the streets of tall, gothic houses they were passing. 'Your mother's house isn't quite as unusual as I'd thought. There seem to be quite a few in the same style.'

'Post-earthquake architecture!' Nick explained. 'San Francisco was rebuilt in the style most fashionable then, and gothic was all the rage in America as well as Europe at that time.'

'I love it, it's so romantic, much lovelier than utility architecture—rows and rows of little boxes! This whole city seems to be built on hills, the streets are so steep. I'd hate to live here if I had to walk anywhere.'

'You wouldn't have to!' Nick said. 'Most people have cars, and of course there are the——'

Before he could finished, Gina gave a little cry of delight. 'Look! A tram! I haven't seen one of them for ages. I'd love to have a ride on one.'

'Cable car,' corrected Nick. 'I was going to say, most people use them to get around if they don't use their own car. You must have heard of them, they're famous.'

'Yes, I suppose I have—but actually seeing them is different. I can't wait to take a ride.'

He smiled at her excitement. 'You'll have to wait until tomorrow, if there's time between appointments. There's no time today. I want to give you some idea of the city. First, the Golden Gate Bridge...'

The limousine suddenly flew over the top of one of the steep hills and Gina gave a gasp, flung sideways.

Nick caught her with one arm and she laughed breathlessly up at him. 'What a weird sensation! That was fun; will we be doing that often?'

'I hope so,' Nick said softly, his arm tightening, and her heart skipped another beat at the look in his eyes.

She wriggled free, thinking ruefully how much she liked him sometimes, when they were together, like this, everything about the *Sentinel* forgotten, the past and all the bad memories blotted out for a while. But she could never forget for long.

The limousine had driven down the steep hills towards the blue sheen of water veiled in the distance by a glistening opalescent mist.

'The bridge is over there,' Nick said. 'But it looks as if you wouldn't get a good view today. Why don't we just go down to Fisherman's Wharf?'

'Fine,' Gina said huskily, and that was what they did. The chauffeur dropped them down at the foot of Taylor Street, and Nick asked him to come back for them in an hour.

Gina stared dreamily at local fishing boats sailing in to dock, a trail of gulls following them and the sunlight glinting on the waves in their wake, then she glanced at some nearby stalls.

'I have to buy presents to take back,' she told Nick. 'That stall has some very pretty costume jewellery. I'd like a closer look.'

She took her time, admiring the necklaces and bangles, the earrings and brooches, before buying some for Roz and Hazel and herself. As she turned away, she stopped, staring out into the bay, open-mouthed.

'Is that...?'

'Yes, Alcatraz,' Nick said, smiling. 'The Rock, they call it—you can go out to the island on a ferry and look around the place. They shut the prison down years ago; 1963, I think. Now it's a sort of museum, but it's pretty eerie, and we don't have time today.'

Gina shivered, staring at the outline of the prison in the faint mist, imagining the cells, the hopeless faces of the prisoners, the sound of keys turning in locks, iron doors slamming. 'I don't think I want to!'

They walked on along Fisherman's Wharf, looking at the many stalls on the sidewalk, the smell of seafood following them all the way; a salty, fresh, smell which gave the place great atmosphere.

'This is great!' she said. 'Maybe we could eat dinner down here one day?'

Nick said, 'If you like, maybe. But there's so much to see and do—later we might get round to visiting the Maritime Museum in Aquatic Park, and I'd like to take you to Hyde Street Pier, they have some wonderful old ships, including a three-masted schooner... I used to love wandering around and imagining what it must have been like to live on one of them at sea for weeks and months on end.'

'Ghastly, I should think!' Gina said teasingly, thinking that it must have been a terribly uncomfortable life.

'All you ever do is have fun at my expense!' Nick said, and she laughed.

'Oh, poor Nick, how sad!'

Then she met his eyes, and her laughter stopped, her green eyes growing shadowy. Nick wasn't joking; he was in deadly earnest and he wasn't thinking about sailing ships. His face held a dangerous mix of anger, desire and bitterness, and Gina's heart gave a convulsive leap.

Oh, Nick, she thought drowningly, and he took a step closer, breathing audibly.

But the cold voice of reason in her head reminded her that she could not trust him, however convincing the look in his eyes.

He never missed an opportunity to get at her. Remember that! she told herself. Whatever they were talking about, sooner or later they were back on the old, familiar track, and Nick was trying again to talk her into giving way to him. She couldn't let him win!

Yet she wanted to cry, a saltiness in her throat, a burning behind her lids.

He was the last man in the world she should love, but one look from him and her body quivered, her mouth grew dry, she was aching to touch and be touched by him.

She shouldn't have come to California with him. He had blackmailed, threatened, used every weapon he had to force her to agree, but whatever he did she should have stood firm, not given in to him.

It was going to be harder than ever, here, away from her safe home territory, to keep him at a distance. She would be living under the same roof, seeing him all the time at work and afterwards, and she was scared of what that would do to her defences. Every time they were alone Nick would make an onslaught on her senses.

The crowds on Fisherman's Wharf swirled around them, but she felt as if they were suddenly as alone as if they were on a desert island.

He was watching her, grey eyes hard and narrowed as they read her shifting expressions.

'Don't!' he said hoarsely, and she shivered.

'Don't what?' she managed, pretending not to know what he meant, and his face tightened and darkened.

'You know very well what! Just now you were smiling at me, there was no shadow in your face, then suddenly you froze up again, and shut me out—and I'm sick of it. Do you hear me? Sick of it!'

The sound of his angry voice made her flinch, paling. She looked around, hoping nobody was listening, but the people strolling past seemed indifferent to them, too concerned in their own lives to bother about anyone else.

'Don't shout at me!' she whispered and Nick audibly ground his teeth.

'Shout at you?' he repeated hoarsely. 'My God, you're lucky I don't hit you. Sometimes I'm so angry with you, I feel like strangling you. One day I'll be pushed too far, Gina, and then…' He paused, breathing thickly. 'I might be driven to taking what you're refusing to give me.'

'Don't threaten me!' she muttered, suddenly fright-

ened. Nick wasn't just talking wildly, not just trying to
scare her. He meant it, she saw, shaken by a look in his
eyes, a darkness which somehow glittered, a rage which
was yet a smouldering, darkly burning desire.

'Frustration can drive men crazy, Gina, be warned,'
he said, then he turned and walked back the way they
had come, leaving her to follow him when her legs had
stopped trembling.

They drove back to his mother's house in silence. Gina
hoped the chauffeur would suppose that they were both
tired, exhausted by walking around for an hour after
their very long flight here from London. To emphasise
that impression she kept her eyes closed for most of
the journey back up to the older part of San Francisco.
The last thing she wanted was for the domestic staff in
the house to gossip about her relationship with Nick.

She wished she knew what his mother imagined that
relationship to be, but she dared not ask Nick. She would
have to wait and see how Mrs Caspian received her.

Conchita opened the front door as they came towards
it. Smiling, she said something in Spanish to Nick, who
nodded calmly, his face under control again, his smile
cool.

'My mother is in the salon, waiting for us,' he told
Gina. 'Do you want to go up to your room first, or join
my mother at once?'

She stammered uncertainly. 'Well ... whichever you
think ...'

He put a hand under her elbow and guided her through
the enormous baronial hall into a cool, high-ceilinged
room.

Gina's nervous eyes skated around, taking in a dazed
impression of glowing, jewel-like colours, the red of
poppies, the green of the sea on a wintry day, pink and
white marble pillars, rich silk curtains, draped and gold-

tasselled, at windows, couches piled with cushions; all
in a Moorish design unlike anything in the rest of the
house. In a large, elegant arched white cage canaries
fluttered and sang. Gina was reminded of the Alhambra
Palace, in Granada, Spain; there was even a stone
fountain, water splashing into a vividly tiled basin, blue
and yellow, with geometric patterns, in the centre of the
room. On a brocade couch lay a woman with Nick's
colouring: olive skin, dark eyes, hair that had once been
jet-black but was now streaked with silver. She must
surely be well past fifty, since Nick himself was in his
late thirties, but her fine eyes and delicately pro-
portioned face still had great beauty. When she was
young she must have been quite breathtaking.

Nick led Gina towards the couch and said in a deep
voice, 'Maman, this is Gina—Gina, my mother.'

A slender hand was extended, the slanting dark eyes
gazed, intently. 'So, you are Gina...' The voice was soft,
lilted with some untraceable accent. Not French, surely?
Yet Mrs Caspian's colouring was distinctly Latin.

Gina offered her own hand, bending. 'It is very kind
of you to invite me to stay in your lovely home, Mrs
Caspian,' she said formally, conscious of the other
woman's perfume; a warm musky scent, exotic, matching
the room.

'I have been looking forward to meeting you for a
long time,' Mrs Caspian said, still holding her hand and
staring up into her face with searching eyes. What was
she looking for? wondered Gina uneasily. What did she
expect to see? Gina's green eyes flickered, her lashes
sweeping down to hide their expression. She was afraid
Nick's mother would see too much in her face, discover
her love for Nick.

He moved a chair closer to the couch. 'Sit down,
Gina—Maman, can I get you a drink?'

'Thank you, darling, I am going to have a *citron pressé*. Conchita will bring a jug of it in a moment.'

He nodded. 'Gina? Will you have home-made lemonade, or something stronger?'

'The same as your mother, if I may,' she murmured, very shy in this amazing room with this extraordinary woman. She wasn't sure what she had been expecting Nick's mother to look like, but she hadn't dreamt that she would be so beautiful, or have such penetrating intelligence in her dark eyes.

'I'll ring Conchita,' said Nick, reaching for the phone, but before he had picked it up it rang shrilly. Nick lifted the receiver and said: 'Yes?' then listened, frowning. 'Oh, very well, Mrs Grant—I'll take it in my study. Would you tell Conchita my mother is ready for her *citron pressé*?'

He put the phone down and glanced apologetically at the two women. 'I'm sorry, I have an urgent business call—I will try to deal with it quickly.'

He walked out of the room with his easy, loping stride, and Gina looked after him with her usual sense of loss whenever they parted. She hated being away from him, and yet she had to keep sending him away. She loved and she hated him. Sometimes she felt as if she was being torn apart.

His mother made a wry little face. 'He is so like his father, much as he would resent it if I said so to him!'

Gina gave her a quick look, at once interested. 'But he seems to have admired his father very much.'

'He admired him and resented him,' Mrs Caspian said. 'My husband was a man with a towering personality— larger than life, rather frightening, especially to children, and even more to his own son. Nick was never sure he could match up to what he thought his father wanted him to be, but he wanted to out-do his father, at the same time. We never have simple reactions to each other, do we?'

'No,' Gina slowly said, and then they both fell silent. Gina looked around her, still trying to absorb the décor, and Mrs Caspian watched her with a smile.

'What do you think of our Arabian fantasy?'

'It's amazing, I've never seen anything like it, except in Spain, in the Alhambra, and they don't have the furniture there—but I'm sure that these couches and curtains and the cage of birds are just what they would have had when the sultans lived there.'

'No, the idea didn't come from Spain, although you're close! The architect, Nathaniel Horner, made several visits to Turkey as a young man, in the late nineteenth century; and his design for this room was based on rooms he saw in palaces in Istanbul. It was this room that made me want this house as soon as I saw it.'

'You look as if you belong here; it's the perfect background for you! It must have been fate that brought you to see the house,' Gina said impulsively, and Mrs Caspian gave her a long, thoughtful look.

'Odd that you should say that, Gina! Fate has played a big part in my life. I don't know if Nick has told you, but I was only seventeen when I was married to his father, and not yet nineteen when Nick was born. The way I met Zachariah was pure fate. My father was Spanish; we were of an old family but we had no money and my parents had too many children. There were eleven of us, seven boys, four girls. Our home was huge and crumbling away, our land was stony, our grapes sour. Then my father met Zachariah Caspian, who was in Spain looking for a country estate, and liked the idea of getting one cheaply. He came to look at our home, met me, and asked my father's consent to our marriage a week later.'

'How romantic!'

'It might have been if I had been in love with him, but I wasn't,' Mrs Caspian said frankly, startling her.

'Oh!' Gina did not know what to say.

'I was seventeen, he was nearly sixty. No, I was not in love, but my father made it plain that I had no choice but to accept. We were desperately poor and Zachariah was very rich. He had been too busy making money to marry but he wanted sons, and unfortunately for me I was rather beautiful when I was young.'

'You still are,' Gina said, and the other woman smiled at her.

'Thank you. You're beautiful yourself, and you have a kind heart, too—I'm not surprised my Nick loves you.'

Gina drew a startled breath, her green eyes wide with shock. What had he told his mother?

Mrs Caspian sighed. 'I've been longing to meet you ever since he told me about you. I badly wanted Nick to find a woman to make him happy, and I was giving up hope that he ever would. His father didn't marry until he was sixty, and I was afraid Nick would put it off for too long, too. Nick looks tough and confident on the outside, but although he has always lived in luxury he didn't have a happy childhood, and I blame myself for that. Not that Nick blames me, or he says he doesn't, but I know that it was my fault. He spent too much time alone, as a child, or with a nanny, and then at boarding-school. He didn't have a real home, for much of the time, he didn't even see much of his sisters...'

'Sisters?' Gina was astonished to hear that Nick had sisters; he never mentioned them.

'Yes, after I had Nick, I had two daughters in quick succession, Lilith, who is thirty-five now, and married, with children of her own, and Alessa, my final child, who is a year younger, and has never married. She is an artist, she paints, and lives in New York on her own.'

'It's strange—Nick never talks about them,' Gina said curiously, and Mrs Caspian sighed.

'Well, I think I understand that. It was after Alessa was born that I quarrelled with my husband and ran away from him. He was a strange man, obsessed with owning things—houses, women, paintings, sculpture, books. He could never have enough of anything, and when I discovered that I wasn't the only woman in his life I left him and came here to California. We had a legal separation, once he accepted that I wasn't coming back— I think by then he no longer wanted me as much as he had when he first met me; he always wanted something new, something different. I had seen this house and fallen in love with it soon after we were married, so Zachariah bought it, there and then. When I left him, I came here—and he agreed to let me live here. When he died he left it to me. We were never divorced. I don't believe in divorce.' She paused, then added practically, 'And, apart from that, I did not want him to have any other son. I didn't want my Nick to have any rivals for his father's estate.'

'You took your children when you left your husband?' Gina asked, wondering what effect the separation had had on Nick.

Mrs Caspian nodded. 'Yes, I left without telling my husband I was going because I knew he would try to stop me taking the children. He didn't want the two girls, he was prepared to let them live with me, but Nick was his only son, and Zachariah fought me for a long time in the courts to get him back, and, of course, he won, because he was one of the richest men in the world and he had the best lawyers. And Nick was his son and only heir.' Her face stiffened with remembered resentment. 'And so I had to give my boy up—and then Zachariah sent him straight off to boarding-school as soon as he got custody. He didn't actually want Nick with him, he just wanted control of him.'

'How old was Nick then?' asked Gina, frowning.

'He was nine. It was hard for him, especially as he knew his sisters were staying with me while he was taken away. He cried and clung to me, and kept saying, "I'll be good, Maman, don't send me away——"' She broke off, close to tears. 'It was the worst day of my life, and of his, too, maybe.'

'Poor little boy,' Gina repeated huskily, blinking back a blur of tears over the picture of him being wrenched out of his mother's arms when he was so young, and taken away to boarding-school. Poor Nick. The story Mrs Caspian had just told her had given her an entirely new idea of him, and she would never take quite the same view of anything he said and did again.

But why had his mother been so astonishingly frank with her? Why had she told her so many intimate details of her life, of Nick's background when they had only just met? She gave Mrs Caspian a wary glance, and the other woman smiled crookedly at her.

'Don't tell Nick I've talked about all this; he almost never mentions those days. For a long time he was difficult with me, for several years after his father took him away from me—Nick blamed me for the breakdown of my marriage, and for his father getting custody. But we talked about it when he got older and he realised it was not as black and white as he had thought it was; nothing ever is! All the same, he hates to talk about it.'

Gina bluntly said, 'Then why did you tell me, Mrs Caspian?'

She got a quick, wry look. 'I knew Nick wouldn't, and I thought you should know why Nick is the way he is!' his mother said.

Gina looked into her dark eyes and understood. Nick had told his mother that Gina would not marry him, and perhaps had told her exactly why—and Mrs Caspian wanted Gina to have more sympathy for Nick. She was hoping that hearing what a troubled childhood he had had might persuade her to forgive him.

CHAPTER NINE

VALERIE was kept very busy that week, and was out of the office so much that she saw nothing of Gib. On Friday she had a lunch appointment with Christa Nordstrom, the Swedish model-turned-film-star, who was filming in Britain, and as she arrived back at Barbary Wharf she saw Gib in the plaza, talking to Sophie Watson by the fountain. Gib was smiling down at Sophie; the girl was gazing up at him, her body language only too readable.

Teeth tight, Valerie averted her eyes and walked on into the building. So, it was OK for Gib to flirt with other girls, but she was supposed to live the life of a nun? He could think again!

There was a note on her desk from Colette Tse, who had already left for the weekend, since the features page was already made up. Valerie skimmed her eyes over the scribbled words. 'Write up an item on Christa before you go home. See you Monday.' Underneath was a list of phone calls Valerie had received while she was out.

Gib's name leapt out from the page. Call timed for eleven-twenty-one. No message.

He had probably rung to ask her to lunch, and, failing to find her, had rung and invited Sophie Watson out instead!

Valerie screwed the paper up and threw it into the bin. It was hard to concentrate that afternoon; jealousy kept stinging like an angry wasp. At three o'clock her phone rang, making her jump. For one second she thought it might be Gib, but it was Guy Faulkner. 'Sorry, Val, but we need to see you again—can you come up?'

'I do have a job to do!' she snapped. 'The features editor asked me to finish this piece urgently.'

'How long will it take you?'

'Another ten minutes,' she crossly admitted.

Guy sounded as if he was smiling. 'Finish it, then, and we'll expect you in a quarter of an hour.'

When Valerie arrived, Sophie was behind her desk in the outer office, and gave Valerie a chilly glance which noted the fashionable cream suit Valerie was wearing, and managed to disparage it without a word.

'They're waiting for you!' she said, turning the remark into an accusation.

'I'm exactly on time!' Valerie coldly said, aware of the other girl's hostile stare on her, as she walked over to the inner door, and tapped.

'Come in!' called Henry Sandel's precise voice.

The first person she saw was Guy in one of his elegant dark pin-striped suits, standing by the window. His thin, clever face was turned towards her, his eyes friendly, but she looked away, without smiling, towards Henry Sandel, who sat behind his desk, the late afternoon sunlight gleaming on his bald, egg-shaped head.

'Ah, Miss Knight,' he said, peering over the gold-framed spectacles balanced on his nose, and stood up to offer her his hand. 'Thank you for coming!'

Guy pulled up a chair for her, and she sat down facing the two men. 'Would you like some tea?' asked Guy.

Valerie was about to refuse when she caught Sophie Watson's eye, sensed the other girl resented the idea of having to make tea for her, and changed her mind.

'Thank you, I'd love some,' she said sweetly.

'Tea for three, Miss Watson,' Henry Sandel told Sophie, who turned on her heel and walked out with a face like thunder.

'Now, Miss Knight,' Henry Sandel said, sitting down again. 'We've heard from Mr Cameron's solicitors and I'm afraid he has not backed down. I had hoped that with mature reflection he might change his mind, but it seems he is determined to go on with his case. Indeed, his lawyer tells me he seems angrier than ever. Before we ourselves engage counsel, therefore, we must be absolutely sure of our ground. Mr Caspian is away at the moment, in California, but I have spoken to him on the telephone and explained how things stand, what our options are. Basically we either print a public apology, withdrawing the statement that Mr Cameron is the father of Miss Green's child, in which case we shall still be liable to pay damages to be fixed out of court, or we defend the case, which will mean a long trial, and if we lose we could find ourselves paying enormous legal costs, for both sides, perhaps—added to whatever exorbitant damages the court may fix.'

Valerie wished he would not keep droning on—she knew the options as well as he did, he did not have to keep explaining them. She wasn't a halfwit. How many times were they going to go through all this?

Guy Faulkner was watching her, amusement in his eyes. As she glanced at him he discreetly winked, his mouth curling at the edges. Valerie looked away again.

'Which is why we asked you to come up and talk to us again,' Henry was intoning. 'I am sorry, Miss Knight, but we must go over your evidence again.'

'OK,' she said, glumly. 'But what else can I tell you? You've got my notebook and tape of the interview, and my report on my further interview with Molly, and all her answers to your queries.'

'I have them here,' he agreed. 'But we can never be too careful, can we?'

'Can't we?'

Guy grinned at the irritation in Valerie's voice, but Henry Sandel looked disapproving.

'No, Miss Knight, we cannot. Ah, here is Miss Watson with the tea. Thank you, yes, I will take a biscuit.' He sipped his tea with a pleasurable sigh. 'Well, we must get down to work—we shall be making a tape-recording of this interview, of course, Miss Knight. For our records. Is that acceptable?'

What was the point of refusing? Valerie nodded.

He almost smiled. 'Well, then, shall we begin? Miss Watson, are you ready?'

For the next two hours, Valerie was given another detailed grilling by Henry Sandel and Guy alternately, and by the time the meeting broke up she was flushed and on the point of snapping.

'Well, I think we've done as much as we usefully can today,' Henry Sandel said, getting up at last. 'Thank you, Miss Knight.'

Did he start every sentence with 'Well...'? Valerie didn't wait around for him to think of something else to ask her; she nodded, and hurried towards the door.

Guy got there first and opened it for her. She muttered, 'Thanks!' without looking.

She sensed his surprise, knew she had been offhand to him, but she was in no mood to be friendly after that gruelling afternoon session. She must not forget that, however charming and friendly he might seem, Guy was a lawyer, and a clever one; and he worked for Nick Caspian. Protecting Caspian International was the essential part of his job. She could not trust him.

But then what man could you trust? The other day Gib had told her, 'You're mine, and you know it!' and

made her promise not to go out with Guy again. Only
a man violently in love would show such jealousy, she
had told herself, and the second she had begun to believe that something catastrophic had happened inside
her. She had admitted finally that she loved Gib, had
loved him for a long time, in spite of herself—in the face
of all reason and common sense. If he hadn't made her
think he was in love with her, she would have gone on
fighting her stupid feelings. How could she have been
so simple-minded?

Just a few days later there was Gib flirting with Sophie
Watson, behind her back, believing her still to be out at
lunch with Christa Nordstrom. Maybe he had been
dating Sophie all the time!

The only comfort Valerie had was that at least she had
not let Gib see how much she cared, how easy it would
be for him to hurt her. It was lucky that she had come
back in time to see him with Sophie, or the next time
she ran into Gib she might have given herself away, be-
trayed by her sensuality, her sheer aching need for the
passion his eyes promised her every time they met.

She pressed the lift button and looked impatiently at
her watch. She wanted to get home, have a long bath,
and relax in front of the television with a snack of something forbidden. Normally she never touched chocolate,
but tonight she craved some.

'Where are you off to in such a hurry?'

She stiffened as Guy came up beside her. 'I'm off home
for the weekend.'

'Come and have a drink first, I want to ask you something,' Guy said, his eyes coaxing.

'Not more questions!' she groaned, walking into the
lift as it arrived.

It was crowded, they had to squeeze into it and with
such a large audience they didn't talk until they reached
the ground floor.

'How are you getting home?' Guy asked.

'Bus,' she said shortly, hurrying.

He kept in step. 'I've got my car—I'll drive you home
and we can talk on the way.'

She might have refused curtly if Sophie Watson had
not walked past them at that instant, moving even faster
and giving them a sideways glance which was carefully
blank.

'Goodnight,' she said in a voice like the cracking of
ice in a glacier.

'Oh, goodnight, Sophie, have a good weekend,' Guy
said casually, seemingly quite unaware of her hostility
to Valerie.

Valerie didn't say anything; she watched the graceful
sway of the other woman's body, sheathed in a tight-
fitting black skirt and matching matador jacket, and
bitterness seeped through her. Sophie was classy, as well
as beautiful. No wonder Gib hadn't been able to resist
her.

Anguish tore at her and she bit down on her lip, afraid
she might cry out. Couldn't you ever be safe from pain?
She had been determined that she was never going to
make a fool of herself again, but love was insidious, it
crept up on you when you weren't looking, and she had
been caught in the same trap for all her wise resolutions.

'You aren't listening!' Guy complained.

'Sorry, what did you say?' Valerie pulled herself
together, struggling to look calm and untroubled.

He gave her a wry little smile. 'I can see you've got
something on your mind. I was asking if you were going
to let me drive you home?'

She took a deep breath. Well, why not? She hadn't had any fun that week, she was fed up and miserable and she wanted to forget about Gilbey Collingwood and this damned lawsuit and everything else in her life that was making her feel like jumping off the roof.

'OK, thank you,' she said, knowing that if he drove her home he would expect her to ask him up for a drink, and maybe more. Well, she would give him a drink, but nothing else. She wasn't to be had for the price of a lift home!

As they drove away from Barbary Wharf they passed Sophie Watson among the throng of office workers making for the Tube station which was a short walk away.

Valerie looked away, watching the dusk falling over the grey river. The days were shortening, autumn was almost upon them.

Had Sophie recognised Guy's car? Noticed her sitting beside him in the front seat? Valerie hoped so. If Sophie saw Gib that weekend she was the type to drop such information casually in conversation; especially if she wasn't sure of him and wanted to wreck any chance that he might still be interested in Valerie.

It wouldn't occur to Sophie that Valerie might want Gib to be told—to get the message that she wasn't his, she could go out with any man she chose, and she didn't care what he thought.

That was not true, of course. She cared, however angrily she resented doing so. But she did not want him to think she did.

'Still preoccupied?' Guy asked, glancing at her as they halted at traffic-lights.

'Sorry,' she said, managing a faint smile.

'Worried about the case?'

'Don't you think I should be?'

He shrugged. 'Don't take too much notice of Henry Sandel. He's paid to be cautious and give nothing away. But you don't really need to worry. I don't think Mr Cameron will bankrupt Caspian International, however greedy he is! And the publicity of the trial will do us no harm at all. Not in this case. He's got a reputation as a ladykiller, which will make his protestations of innocence very suspect, and Molly Green is God's gift to a picture desk. The buying public will take one look at that sweet little innocent, and clamour for Mac Cameron to do right by her. With this story, we're on the side of the angels, in spite of what Henry Sandel seems to think. He knows the law upside-down, but he's no judge of what sells newspapers. You'll probably make your name, and get fat offers from other papers, which I hope you'll refuse, the *Sentinel* will take a huge leap in circulation and Mr Caspian will be so happy, he'll double your salary.'

She laughed. 'That'll be the day!'

'Maybe that is a slight exaggeration, but your job isn't likely to be at risk, especially if we win the case.'

'Not if—when!' she insisted. 'But thanks for cheering me up, anyway.'

They drew up outside her apartment block, and she smiled at him. He had done his best to make her feel better, and she was grateful enough to ask, 'Would you like to come in for a drink?'

'If you'll agree to have dinner with me afterwards,' he said and she hesitated, realising that if she accepted the invitation she would be getting more involved with him. Guy Faulkner was good company and he had been kind this evening, but she didn't want a closer relationship with him. There was already one man too many in her life.

'I'm really rather tired this evening,' she apologised.

'But you'll want to eat, surely?' coaxed Guy, oozing charm from every pore. 'Why not with me? We can go somewhere near by, somewhere quick and simple, but good, then I'll drop you back here and you can get to bed early.'

Valerie couldn't help laughing. 'You should be a barrister. You're horribly persuasive—I can just imagine you in court, sweet-talking a jury into letting your clients get away with murder.'

'Is that a yes?' he enquired and she sighed and nodded.

'Against my better judgement, yes. But only because I feel I owe it to you for reassuring me about the Cameron case. It has been keeping me awake at nights, worrying about the future.'

When it wasn't worry over the threat of a lawsuit keeping her awake, it was worry over Gilbey Collingwood! she thought grimly. At this moment she was beset with problems.

Guy came up to her flat to have a drink and wait for her to take a quick shower and change her clothes.

'Have a look through my compact discs, play any you like,' she said, after she had poured him a whisky and ginger ale, and while she was towelling herself after her shower she heard jazz floating through the flat.

Another sound cut into that a second later—her telephone was ringing.

'Shall I answer that?' called Guy.

'Thanks,' she called back. 'Say I'm in the shower and take any message; say I'll call back later, if it's important.'

The ringing stopped. She put on her towelling robe and was just leaving the bathroom when Guy called, 'I think you'd better take this call, Val. It's Gilbey Collingwood; he says Molly Green has gone into labour.'

Valerie ran barefoot down the corridor and took the phone from him. 'Hello?' she said breathlessly.

'Showering after making love, are you?' Gib asked with bitter sarcasm.

She didn't bother to answer that. 'What's all this about Molly being in labour?' she demanded instead.

He laughed humourlessly, then said in businesslike tones, 'She started having pains this afternoon, but thought they were indigestion because the baby isn't due for another six weeks, but they didn't stop, they got worse, so her cousins drove her to the nearest maternity hospital and she was admitted two hours ago.'

Valerie was stunned, but her mind hadn't stopped working just because she was so taken aback.

'Who told you?' she asked, following the training she had been given as a cub reporter—first check your source!

'Her cousin Janet,' Gib curtly told her.

'She rang you? Why on earth did she do that? How did she have your number?'

'She didn't,' he said. 'She rang you, at your office, but you weren't there. Whoever answered the phone told her you were busy with the legal department.' His voice held a sneer. 'They weren't kidding, were they?'

An angry flush kindled her cheeks. 'Cut the cheap jokes, will you?'

'I'm glad you think it's a joke,' said Gib. 'My sense of humour doesn't quite stretch that far.'

'Look,' she said through her teeth, so angry that her voice was thick and blurred, 'just tell me how you end up being the messenger!'

'Are you drunk?' he asked and her flush deepened.

'No, I'm not!'

'You sound drunk!' he muttered.

'Well, I'm not. I haven't had anything to drink since lunchtime, and even then I was on mineral water except for one glass of champagne just to keep Christa Nordstrom company. And stop deliberately changing the subject. How do you come to be the one to ring me?'

'It's very simple. Janet left a message for you, and a telephone number where you could ring her. Someone scribbled you a note, and left it on your desk, and that is where I read it. I suppose whoever wrote the note was expecting you to come back some time, but you obviously went straight home.' His voice took on that stinging note again. 'In a hurry to get to bed, were you?'

'Don't start that again!'

There was a brief silence, then he added, 'Janet hadn't said why she needed to talk to you so I rang her, and when she explained that the baby was on the way I promised to get in touch with you and get you down there.'

Valerie's deep blue eyes widened in startled surprise. 'What? Why on earth should I go down there?'

'Molly is having a bad time, according to Janet. In a lot of pain and needing constant company, a lot of comforting and reassurance.'

Valerie gave a sigh. 'Poor kid. But, even so—she won't want me there! I've only met her a few times.'

'She likes you and trusts you,' Gib said tersely. 'She would never have poured her heart out to you if she didn't. Why else has Janet rung to tell you Molly was having the baby? She thought you would want to know, want to be there.' His tone sharpened again, slashing at her like a knife. 'What's the matter? Enjoying yourself so much you can't bear to leave him?'

'What if I am?' she bit back, hating him enough to let him think what he liked.

'That's too bad!' Gib snapped. 'But your job has to
come first; it always has until now! OK, you won't come
because you like Molly, and care what happens to her,
but you're still going to have to come because the *Sentinel*
must be the first to get this story. This baby is the
Sentinel's baby, in more ways than one, and they are
going to go to town on it. They'll want pictures—you
had better arrange that with the picture desk. How long
will it take you to get dressed?'

'Five minutes. It will take me hours to drive down
there, though.' She groaned. 'And I'm tired and hungry
after a difficult day. The last thing I want to do is drive
all that way, especially at night. I hate driving in the
dark.'

'You won't need to—I'm driving you down there. I
promised Janet I would, and I intend to.'

Alarm flashed through her and she angrily began, 'No,
you won't! I can perfectly well——'

The phone went dead. He had hung up. She hung up,
too, biting her lip, and turned to find Guy lounging
behind her, a glass in his hand and a curious expression
on his thin face. She couldn't quite make out whether
he was angry or amused.

'I'm sorry, Guy, but——'

'You're driving to this hospital, I know. Do I gather
that Collingwood plans to drive you down there?' he
asked in a dry voice.

'I can drive myself,' Valerie said crossly.

'I'll be happy to drive you,' Guy murmured, watching
her intently.

'I wouldn't dream of——'

'I want to, Val,' he cut across her protest, his voice
level and decided, and she bit her lip, looking away, the
flush on her cheekbones growing.

'Oh! That's very kind . . . I am grateful, really, but . . .'
Her voice trailed off, she gave him another quick,
nervous, helpless look, and he smiled crookedly.

'I see. I had the idea Collingwood was chasing you
hard and you didn't like him but weren't sure how to
get the message home. My mistake, obviously.'

Valerie opened her mouth to tell him he wasn't mis-
taken, that was exactly the situation, but somehow the
words would not come out.

Guy calmly smoothed the moment out, talking quietly.
'You'd better go and get dressed, I'll let myself out. I
hope everything goes well for Molly. The *Sentinel* will
certainly want to carry the news about the baby being
born. Our readers are hooked on the continuing story.
While you're down there, arrange a blood-test for the
baby. We're going to need that if this case isn't settled
out of court.'

He drained his glass and moved to the front door, and
Valerie politely went with him, one hand holding the
lapels of her towelling robe close to her throat.

'I'm sorry,' she said huskily, and he nodded, his mouth
twisting.

'Some you win, some you lose,' he murmured ob-
scurely, then bent to kiss her, very quickly and lightly.

A second later he had gone and she closed the door,
putting a trembling hand on her lips. She hardly knew
Guy, yet she felt troubled, as if a door which was just
opening had suddenly been closed again, for ever.

But she had no time to stand there, wondering about
Guy Faulkner. She ran down the corridor and began to
dress hurriedly, in pale blue denim jeans and a sleeveless
top over which she pulled a peacock-blue sweater. It was
a long drive to Devon, and the night might turn very
cold.

She spent five minutes packing an overnight bag, too, because she wouldn't want to drive back to London until tomorrow, and might even stay all weekend, depending on Molly's condition.

The doorbell rang, making her heart turn over. He was here. She snatched up her bag and made for the door.

'You dressed fast. Where's Faulkner?' Gib asked coldly, running narrowed eyes down over her.

She came out, closing the door behind her. 'Home, by now, I expect. And I can drive myself, I don't need you!'

'Oh, don't you?' he threw back in a sort of snarl, and she flinched, her nerves on edge.

'Especially if you're going to snap at me all the way there!'

She walked away and Gib caught up with her, his hand closing on her arm. 'My car is outside.'

'My car is in my garage!' She tried to pull free, but he wouldn't let her.

'I'm driving you!' He hustled her out of the building just as one of her neighbours was coming home. Valerie pulled a smile over her flushed face.

'Good evening, Mrs Bridge.'

'Good evening. Turning quite chilly, isn't it? Well, I suppose we must expect it—the summer's really over,' the other woman murmured, giving Gib the fluttering glance of a woman who was growing old, but still appreciated a good-looking man.

'Yes, and you mustn't stand out here, catching cold,' Gib said, giving her a brief smile. 'Come along, Val, we have a long drive ahead of us.'

'Going somewhere nice?' Mrs Bridge asked, looking down at Valerie's overnight bag with beady eyes.

'No, it's just work,' said Valerie, letting Gib take her bag and put it into the back of his car, but as they drove away she saw Mrs Bridge watching them from the window of her ground-floor flat.

'She suspects we're off on a wicked weekend,' Gib mockingly said, and laughed.

'It isn't funny!' she said, glaring. 'I don't want to get that sort of reputation!'

'What sort have you got now?' he asked nastily. 'I'm sure she has noticed Faulkner coming and going.'

'That was the first time——' Valerie began, then broke off, biting her lip. 'Oh, why should I bother? You have no right to lecture me, anyway—you, of all people!'

He turned his head to look sharply at her. 'What does that mean?'

They were driving round a sharp bend and the car drifted towards the centre of the road, almost hitting another vehicle coming from the opposite direction.

'Keep your eyes on the road!' Valerie stammered, terrified for a second, then the other driver screeched past, his horn blaring, and Gib pulled his car back into the right traffic lane.

They drove on in silence for a while, then Valerie suddenly thought of something, her dark blue eyes widening.

'We should have rung Mac Cameron!'

'You're kidding!' Gib said, and laughed shortly. 'If he refuses to admit the baby is his he won't want to know it's being born!'

She couldn't deny that, and sighed. 'I suppose you're right. That's so sad. And puzzling. I wish I knew the truth. It's so confusing—Gina Tyrrell says he's genuine, she can't believe he's lying about not being the father. He was really upset about Molly, as if she had hurt him badly by accusing him. But, at the same time, I like Molly a lot, and I can't believe Molly is lying.'

'One of them has to be!'

'Yes,' she wryly conceded. 'But whichever it is, it isn't the baby's fault, poor little mite. It's being born in the middle of a war, which it knows nothing about.' She looked at the clock on his dashboard. It was almost eight o'clock! 'By now it might have been born, in fact! What time do you think we'll get there?'

'Not much before eleven,' Gib said. 'But, judging by what Molly's cousin said, they don't expect the baby to arrive much before midnight. Have you eaten tonight?'

'No, we were just going out to dinner.'

'Making love gives you an appetite, does it?' Gib sniped, and she gave him an angry look.

'We didn't make love! And don't start that again! I am not driving all the way to Devon with you taking bites out of me every other mile.'

He laughed curtly. 'It must be because I'm hungry. We'll stop and eat somewhere along the road—it will have to be fast food; there's no time for a three-course meal.'

They turned off the motorway half an hour later and found an Indian restaurant on the edge of a small town.

They were the only customers; the friendly waiter told them as he opened their bottle of wine that people usually ate there later, after the pubs closed or after seeing a film.

'Now it is nice and quiet for you,' he said, with an encouraging glance, as if suspecting them of being lovers, and put on a tape of Indian love-songs before vanishing into the kitchen, perhaps to help the cook who was preparing their food. Valerie sipped her glass of wine, looking around. The restaurant had dark blue velvet curtains hanging at the windows, the walls had a wooden trellis nailed over a wallpaper printed with trailing green leaves, and the ceiling was painted dark blue, with silver stars and a silver crescent moon stuck on to it.

'Amazing décor,' she commented, and Gib glanced up and laughed.

'Very romantic.' He drank some more of his wine, watching the red swirl of it in his glass, then said abruptly without looking up, 'I'm at the end of my rope, Val. I can't take much more.'

Her breathing almost stopped. She couldn't get a sound out, her ears deafened with the sound of her own heartbeat.

'I really began to think you cared, that at last you felt the way I did!' Gib muttered, and through her lashes she watched his fingers clenching on the stem of his wine glass. 'And then you start dating Faulkner! Why?' His voice thickened, harsh and bitter, his head lifted and he shot her a look, his eyes dark. 'Are you getting some sort of kick out of hurting me?'

'I'm not like that!'

'Aren't you? For months you've had me dancing on a piece of string, you wouldn't say yes and you wouldn't say no...'

'That's not true! I told you I never dated married men!'

'And I told you my marriage had been over for years, and I was only waiting for a divorce!'

'And while you were waiting you dated half the girls in the company!'

'I took the odd girl out now and then, OK. It never went further than a casual date. I took them out to dinner, or to a show, went to office parties with them. It was a friendly arrangement—they knew the score and so did I. At the end of the evening, I saw them home and said goodnight on their doorstep.'

'What about Sophie?'

'Sophie?' repeated Gib. 'Sophie Watson, you mean? What about her?'

Angrily, Valerie said, 'I've seen the two of you together!' She felt a stab of wild pain, of fierce jealousy. 'I've seen the way she looks at you! And I know she can't stand the sight of me—I'm not stupid, you know!'

Gib's sinewy hands shot out and caught hers, and the touch made her gasp, a shiver running down her spine. She looked up, dark blue eyes huge and glowing, and he gazed into them, his face intent, a glitter of what looked dangerously like triumph in his own eyes.

'I don't know what the hell you're talking about, but if you imagine that I'm having an affair with Sophie Watson you're crazy. Are you admitting you were jealous, Val?'

His voice stopped as the waiter came through the swing doors from the kitchen carrying a tray loaded with their meal. Gib let go of her hands and leaned back, breathing as if he had been running. Valerie picked up her wine glass and tried to drink a little, but her hands were shaking too much, so she put the glass down again untouched.

The waiter laid out their food, gave them plates, re-filled their glasses, then discreetly left again, no doubt picking up the charged atmosphere between them. His tact was wasted, however. Five minutes later, a large party arrived, the waiter returned, and the room was filled with noise; voices and laughter and the clink of bottles.

Gib and Valerie ate without saying a word, hardly looking at each other. They had coffee and left well within the hour Gib had suggested for their stop.

Instead of driving straight back on to the motorway, though, Gib parked in a country lay-by, under rustling

sycamore trees whose leaves were turning gold and
blowing away on every breath of wind.

'Why have you stopped?' Valerie whispered, her heart
beating so loudly that she could barely hear herself speak.

He turned, one arm going along the back of the seat,
behind her head, his eyes burning in the darkness of the
car.

'I've got you alone, for the first time in ages,' he said
softly. 'Nobody is going to interrupt us this time, and I
want absolute honesty from you at last, Val. If you were
jealous over Sophie, it has to mean something...'

She flushed hotly. 'I didn't say I was jealous!'

He ignored the denial. 'And the only thing it could
mean is that you do love me, whether you admit it or
not. Did you go out with Guy Faulkner just to get back
at me because you thought I was seeing Sophie?'

Her eyes slid away, and Gib laughed huskily.

'You're crazy. How many times do I have to tell you
I love you, and I want to marry you?'

In anguish, Valerie cried out, 'But how long would it
last? You've been married before, and that didn't last
long, did it? Oh, I know you say your marriage was a
mistake and you're much older and wiser and wouldn't
make that mistake again, but how do I know you won't
walk out on me, too? My father left my mother and it
wrecked our lives. I don't want to do that to a child of
mine. I want to have children, but I want to be sure I
can give them a stable home, with loving parents—not
have to watch them going through what I went through.
A divorce is like an earthquake—suddenly there's this
terrible split in the earth you stand on and you can't
jump across the abyss in between—you're stuck on one
side, with one parent, and the other parent drifts away.
Nothing is ever the same again afterwards. I grew up
not trusting men, not trusting my own feelings, not

wanting to love anyone in case they didn't go on loving me, in case I got hurt!'

Gib framed her face with his hands, staring into her eyes. 'We all get hurt sooner or later, Val. It will hurt intolerably if you send me away. Life doesn't give us guarantees. An earthquake is a natural event, the insurance companies call it an Act of God, and there's no insurance that will cover it. Human beings can't insure against getting hurt, either. I can only keep saying that I love you and I've loved you already for what seems a very long time. Heaven knows you've tried to stop me loving you, but it didn't work. I think we could be happy together, if only you give me a chance to prove it.'

She looked at the strong, sure lines of his face, and trembled. 'I want to, Gib, but...'

'Ah!' he breathed, as if she had struck him. 'Val. Wanting to is all it takes. Don't be a little coward—tell me you love me. I've got to hear you say it.'

His eyes held hers, giving her the courage to whisper what she had only just realised herself. 'I love you.' Her mouth was dry with the terror of admitting it aloud, but when it was said the world didn't come to an end, and she didn't regret having said it. He was looking at her with so much feeling that she almost fainted.

'I love you,' she said again, in a stronger voice, and then: 'Darling...oh, darling...' Passion was burning deep inside her like a peat fire, darkly secret, smoky, smouldering on and on for ever.

He closed his eyes, and she felt a shudder run through his whole body. 'I can't believe you've said it,' he muttered. 'It is true, isn't it, Val?' Then his head came down, her lips parted under the desire of his kiss, and she forgot everything else but the satisfaction of that driving necessity she had been trying to suppress for so long.

Waves of sensuality crashed over her as his hands caressed and explored; she had not expected her body to react so fiercely, with such need, clinging, trembling. For the first time in her life Valerie abandoned all control, moaning in pleasure as she kissed him back, stroking his cheek, the nape of his neck, her fingers twisting wildly in his hair, her hands running down his back, pulling him closer to her.

Groaning, he responded to every touch, every movement; he was darkly flushed and shuddering, all sense of time and place lost in the intensity of their lovemaking, and it was a shock to both of them when another car drove into the lay-by, headlights suddenly lighting up the inside of Gib's car, making the lovers leap apart.

Gib swore. Blinded, and dazed, Valerie fell back in her seat, trembling.

'Now that...' Gib said in a husky, shaky voice, '...that was an earthquake! And a massive one, too. I'm lucky to be alive.'

She laughed a little wildly. 'Me too.'

Gib gave her a crooked smile, his eyes tender. 'Well, I hate to say this, but, much as I'd like to stay here with you all night, we had better drive on if we want to get to the hospital before Molly has the baby.'

'Oh! I'd forgotten Molly!' she gasped, so horrified that she made him laugh as he started his car again.

They arrived just before midnight, in the end, and found Molly's cousins half asleep in the waiting-room of the hospital. They sat up, blinking and yawning, with rumpled hair and flushed faces.

'Oh, hello!' said Janet. 'You came, after all. Molly's father said you wouldn't come all this way, and I shouldn't have rung you.'

'How is she? Has she had the baby?' Valerie asked urgently, and they shook their heads with sober faces.

'Not yet. Her parents are in there—the midwife turned us out when they arrived, they didn't want too many people in the room. It isn't going well, I'm afraid they may have to do a Caesarean.'

'Oh, no! Poor Molly!' Both Janet and Andy looked exhausted, and Valerie wondered how Molly must be looking. 'How long has she been in labour?'

Before Janet could answer that the door swung open again and they all turned. Molly's father staggered into the room, his collar open, his tie off, his hair ruffled but a smile on his pale face.

'Has she had it?' Janet burst out and he looked at her dazedly.

'Aye, a tiny little girl, only four pounds, they've put her in an incubator, but they said her heart was strong, she's going to be OK.' He sat down on the nearest chair and ran his hands through his hair. 'I am so tired. I don't know how you women stand this. I never want to go through another night like it.'

'How's Molly?' asked Valerie, and he looked at her blankly, as if he didn't recognise her.

'They gave her an injection, and she's sleeping. My wife has gone off to the cloakroom to have a good cry alone. I feel like joining her.'

Janet laughed. 'You need a strong cup of sweet tea.'

'I need a real drink,' he said. 'And all the pubs are shut! When I get home I shall have a stiff whisky, I can tell you!'

'As it happens, I have a flask in my jacket,' said Gib, producing a leather-bound flask from a pocket. 'I had a feeling it might come in handy tonight.'

'God bless you!' Mr Green said, eyes brightening.

Gib took a paper cup from the coffee machine near by, poured a good finger of whisky into it and gave it to Mr Green. While he was drinking it, Valerie whispered to Janet, 'I suppose nobody rang Mac Cameron and told him?'

Mr Green picked up the question, in spite of her care to speak softly, and swung round, glaring. 'No, we have not! And we don't want him here. If he showed his face I'd be tempted to kill him.'

Valerie understood his anger, but she couldn't help thinking of Molly's unhappy eyes, and the little girl who had just come into the world without a father. It was all such a muddle. But was Mac Cameron her father? The puzzle of the situation struck her again, and she sighed.

Gib was watching her. He put an arm round her. 'You're tired; you need a night's rest. Come on.' He turned towards the others. 'If Molly is asleep we won't be able to see her now. We'll find a hotel and check in for the night, and come back tomorrow, with your permission.'

'You won't get a hotel to take you at this hour,' Janet told them. 'Come back with us, stay at the farm.'

'Are you sure?' Valerie asked uncertainly. It was probably true that they wouldn't be accepted by a hotel, arriving so late at night, but she hated to impose on these people.

'Of course,' Janet insisted. 'We have plenty of room. We're just leaving, and you can follow our car to the farm.'

Valerie and Gib walked out some minutes later into a chill autumn night, the skies very clear and the stars as bright as fire. Looking up at them, Valerie shivered.

Gib's arm tightened on her. 'What?'

'I feel so sorry for Molly and her baby.'

'Molly has loving parents, and friends who care about her—you don't need to worry about her.'

'The future is very uncertain for her, though—and for her baby. What if we lose this case? Molly wouldn't get an allowance from Mac Cameron, and she would have to bring up the baby without help.'

'We'll cross that bridge when we come to it. Stop fretting yourself over what might be—and concentrate on us.' Gib kissed her tenderly, lingeringly, his fingers stroking her cheek. 'You played hard to get for a long time, but I've got you now, and I will make you happy. You'll see.'

Don't miss *A Sweet Addiction*, Barbary Wharf Book Five.

Someone is lying, but is it Mac Cameron or Molly Green?
Will Gina decide to continue her relationship with Mac
now that she's seeing Nick in a new light? And who will
Guy Faulkner turn to next, now that he's lost Valerie
to Gib?

Find out in *A Sweet Addiction*, Barbary Wharf Book Five,
coming next month from Harlequin Presents.

TB2

HARLEQUIN ✦ PRESENTS®

BARBARY WHARF

Charlotte Lamb is one of Harlequin's best-loved and bestselling authors. Her extraordinary career, in which she has written more than one hundred books, has helped shape the face of romance fiction around the world.

Born in the East End of London, Charlotte spent her early childhood moving from relative to relative to escape the bombings of World War II. After working as a secretary in the BBC's European department, she married a political reporter who wrote for the *Times*. Charlotte recalls that it was at his suggestion that she began to write "because it was one job I could do without having to leave our five children." Charlotte and her family now live in a beautiful home on the Isle of Man. It is the perfect setting for an author who creates characters and stories that delight romance readers everywhere.

BARBARY WHARF
#1498 BESIEGED
#1509 BATTLE FOR POSSESSION
#1513 TOO CLOSE FOR COMFORT

"BARBARY WHARF" SWEEPSTAKES
OFFICIAL RULES — NO PURCHASE NECESSARY

1. To enter each drawing complete the appropriate Offical Entry Form. Alternatively, you may enter any drawing by hand printing on a 3" × 5" card (mechanical reproductions are not acceptable) your name, address, daytime telephone number and prize for which that entry is being submitted (Wedgwood Tea Set, $1,000 Shopping Spree, Sterling Silver Candelabras, Royal Doulton China, Crabtree & Evelyn Gift Baskets or Sterling Silver Tray) and mailing it to: Barbary Wharf Sweepstakes, P.O. Box 1397, Buffalo, NY 14269-1397.

No responsibility is assumed for lost, late or misdirected mail. For eligibility all entries must be sent separately with first class postage affixed and be received by 11/23/92 for Wedgwood Tea Set (approx. value $543) or, at winner's option, $500 cash drawing; 12/22/92 for the $1,000 Shopping Spree at any retail establishment winner selects or, at winner's option, $1,000 cash drawing; 1/22/93 for Sterling Silver Candelabras (approx. value $875) or, at winner's option, $700 cash drawing, 2/22/93 for the Royal Doulton China service for 8 (approx. value $1,060) or, at winner's option, $900 cash drawing; 3/22/93 for the 12 monthly Crabtree & Evelyn Gift Baskets (approx. value $960) or, at winner's option, $750 cash drawing and, 4/22/93 for the Sterling Silver Tray (approx. value $1,200) or, at winner's option, $750 cash drawing. All winners will be selected in random drawings to be held within 7 days of each drawing eligibility deadline.

A random drawing from amongst all eligible entries received for participation in any or all drawings will be held no later than April 29, 1993 to award the Grand Prize of a 10 day trip for two (2) to London, England (approx. value $6,000) or, at winner's option, $6,000 cash. Travel option includes 10 nights accommodation at the Kensington Park Hotel, Continental breakfast daily, theater tickets for 2, plus round trip airfare and $1,000 spending money; air transportation is from commercial airport nearest winner's home; travel must be completed within 12 months of winner notification, and is subject to space and accommodation availability; travellers must sign and return a Release of Liability prior to traveling.

2. Sweepstakes offer is open only to residents of the U.S. (except Puerto Rico), and Canada who are 21 years of age or older, except employees and immediate family members of Torstar Corp., its affiliates, subsidiaries, and all agencies, entities and persons connected with the use, marketing, or conduct of this sweepstakes. All federal, state, provincial, municipal and local laws apply. Offer void wherever prohibited by law. Taxes and/or duties are the sole responsibility of the winner. Any litigation within the province of Quebec respecting the conduct and awarding of a prize may be submitted to the Régie des loteries et courses du Quebec. All prizes will be awarded; winners will be notified by mail. No substitution of prizes is permitted. Winner selection is under the supervision of D.L. Blair, Inc., an independent judging organization whose decisions are final. Chances of winning in any drawing are dependent upon the number of eligible entries received. All prizes are valued in U.S. currency.

3. Potential winners must sign and return an Affidavit of Eligibility within 30 days of notification. In the event of non-compliance within this time period, the prize may be awarded to an alternate winner. Any prize or prize notification returned as undeliverable may result in the awarding of that prize to an alternate winner. By acceptance of their prize, winners consent to the use of their names, photographs or their likenesses for purposes of advertising, trade and promotion on behalf of Torstar Corp. without further compensation to the winner unless prohibited by law. Canadian winners must correctly answer a time-limited arithmetical question in order to be awarded a prize.

4. For a list of winners (available after 5/31/93), send a separate stamped, self-addressed envelope to: Barbary Wharf Sweepstakes Winners, P.O. Box 4526, Blair, NE 68009.

This month's special prize:

Royal Doulton China Service for 8!

Imagine how proud you'll feel serving dinner on this exquisite porcelain from Royal Doulton, admired the world over as the finest English china. If you're the winner you'll receive a service for eight in the Terrace Hill pattern, plus a sugar bowl, creamer, serving bowl and platter. Each place setting includes dinner plate, salad plate, soup bowl, cup and saucer.

The Grand Prize:

An English Holiday for Two!

Visit London and tour the neighborhoods where the characters in *Barbary Wharf* work and fall in love. Visit the fabulous shops, the museums, the Tower of London and Buckingham Palace. . .enjoy theater and fine dining. And as part of your ten-day holiday, you'll be invited to lunch with the author, Charlotte Lamb! Round-trip airfare for two, first-class hotels, and meals are all included.

BARBARY WHARF

SWEEPSTAKES

OFFICIAL

ENTRY FORM

THIS MONTH'S SPECIAL PRIZE:

Royal Doulton China, Service for 8

NOTICE》 Entry must be received by February 22, 1993. Winner will be notified by March 2, 1993.

GRAND PRIZE:

A Vacation to England!

See prize descriptions on the back of this entry form.

Fill in your name and address below and return this entry form with your invoice in the reply envelope provided. Good luck!

NAME

ADDRESS

CITY   STATE/PROV.   ZIP/POSTAL CODE

(   )

DAYTIME PHONE NUMBER   (AREA CODE)

BW-M4